Blackface Stallion

HELEN GRIFFITHS

Blackface Stallion

Illustrated by Victor Ambrus

HOLIDAY HOUSE · NEW YORK

Library of Congress Cataloging in Publication Data

Griffiths, Helen.
Blackface stallion.

SUMMARY: Follows the life of a wild horse living in
the desert of northern Mexico as he grows from a foal to
a magnificent stallion with a herd of his own.
1. Wild horses—Legends and stories. [1. Wild
horses—Fiction. 2. Horses—Fiction] I. Ambrus, Victor G. II. Title.
PZ10.3.G8808Bl   [Fic]   80-15850
ISBN 0-8234-0420-X

For my daughter Cristina
who asked me for a horse story
that was only about horses

AUTHOR'S NOTE

In order to describe the life of the wild horse as accurately as possible it was necessary for me to do quite a lot of research. So much written about wild horses is based on imagination rather than observation that it isn't always easy to distinguish fact from fiction. Of the varied sources of information, one book in particular I feel it necessary to mention, as without it, I don't think Blackface's story could have been written at all. This is *Mustangs: A Return to the Wild* by Hope Ryden, published by The Viking Press in 1972.

CONTENTS

The Palomino

I

The State of Chihuahua, north-west Mexico, early summer 1956, and a dirt road full of holes and rocks, hardly improved upon since the Spaniards passed that way some four hundred years earlier. It was the nearest thing to a main highway in that part of the world, this track that connected one lonely *rancho* to another – an artery fed from time to time by other dirt roads, some of which petered out among overgrowing mesquite and prickly pear because no wheels had passed that way to crush them. To the west lay the Sierra Madre mountains from which the small truck on the road was travelling, heading south-eastward across the desert, with still a long way to go.

Villa, the driver, had his foot on the accelerator in spite of the dips and curves, the holes and the rocks. He was used to the dusty, bumpy tracks that characterized this part of the country, but didn't like them and was anxious to get through the desert as soon as possible. Sweat tickled in the creases round his neck. If he reduced speed the cabin became an unbearable oven, even with the windows open. He almost envied the horse carried at the back. Perhaps her journey wasn't too comfortable – several times she had been thrown off balance, banging her hips and shoulders against the boards – but at least she had the benefit of whatever breeze the truck's movement generated.

Perhaps Don Rafael wouldn't be happy at the way his mare was getting knocked about, not that in Villa's opinion it was likely to do her much harm. What were a few cuts and bruises compared with this accursed heat? He wasn't making much out of this journey so the sooner he was through with it the better.

Villa wasn't interested in horses, knew nothing about them, and this was the first time he had been persuaded to take a horse aboard. It was only because Don Rafael was a friend of his. He had such a bee in his bonnet about having the mare covered by some special stallion he had heard about that even the two hundred miles across some of the toughest terrain in the state wouldn't stop him.

Villa himself didn't know where all these tracks led to, if they led anywhere. There was no reliable map of the area. People just got to recognize landmarks and kept them in their memory. His truck was one of the few that kept the roads from returning to the wilderness. Some villages only twenty miles from each other were as much separated by unexplored, cactus-covered, thorn-strewn desert as if a mighty ocean intervened, and no one with any sense ever took to these parts unless they had good cause. Villa's cause was money. Don Rafael's ambition was to get a first class colt or filly from a renowned quarter-horse stallion and his palomino mare. In the truck-driver's opinion Don Rafael was crazy, but what were an old man's horse dreams to him? This was just one more trip – the longest he had ever undertaken, to be sure – carrying whatever he was paid to carry, and he never drove any slower than he had to. He hardly even reduced speed to swing down an incline where the track had all but disappeared.

Then several things happened at once. A front tire exploded as it ran over an agave spine sharper than any nail; the truck spun out of control, careened against a rock and was flung on to its side by the force of impact; Villa's head crashed through the windscreen, and Don Rafael's golden mare was shot through yards of scrub which tore half the skin off her flank and back before she came to a halt. Had she been tied to the truck rails she would have had her neck broken. As it was, after a few minutes, she was able to struggle dazedly to all fours. Villa never moved again.

2

Don Rafael's mare was one of the prettiest palominos anyone could hope to see, her colour perfectly even, reminiscent of the gold which had brought the *conquistadores* and their horses to this land so long ago; her mane and tail like fresh milk. She hadn't always been so beautiful. He had found her in a street in Chihuahua city, the property of an ignorant peasant who had her pulling a heavily laden cart while she was only a two-year-old. She was overworked, half starved, her soft lips and gums rubbed raw by an ill-fitting rusty bit, her coat tatty and staring, a travesty of gold.

No one but Don Rafael would have given her a second glance, and even he might have passed her by had not the sun on that particular afternoon shone on her miserable, dried-up hide in such a way that, all of a sudden, he saw what she really was, what she ought to be. He bought her there and then, took her back to his little ranch in the Sierra Madre, nursed her like a long-lost grand-daughter and dreamed of the day when she would be strong and beautiful like the golden palomino he had mounted in his youth.

It took a long time for her to grow strong; she was under-sized and weak from bad feeding and strain; but she began to shine after only a few weeks. When her sores had healed, the galls disappeared and the flesh filled out, some of his dream seemed likely to come true. But as time passed he realized she would never be quite what he had hoped for.

Her spirit was broken. She was mild, gentle, submissive,

14

but she had no will of her own. Without any will, she seemed to lack even the most elementary intelligence. Fear had driven all capability of learning from her. Brute force was all she seemed able to understand but Don Rafael was as incapable of using force on her as he was of giving up in despair. He treated her like a pet dog, abandoned any attempt to ride her, talked to her of days gone by and his hopes for the future, and when she was a five-year-old, beautiful and gleaming, with no signs now of her miserable past, he led her up a ramp into Villa's truck and sent her on her way to the golden quarter-horse stallion, who might yet get him a colt that would make his dream come true. . . .

A pair of buzzards came to sit near the palomino while she stood amid the scrub which had both torn and saved her, drawn by the smell of blood that seeped patchily from exposed flesh. They weren't close enough to frighten her, settling on a nearby rock. Several vultures came to perch on the roof of the truck but moved off quickly, their claws burnt by the hot metal.

The afternoon went slowly by, the palomino gradually recovering from shock as shadows grew longer with the westering sun. The memory of a man with a bucket of feed standing at the corral gate reminded her of what she must do. Go over to him, listen to his voice, feel his hands, then eat. But there was no corral, no man, no feed.

It took great hunger to get the mare moving and, when she did finally decide to go and look for Don Rafael or her feed, or both, her pace was stiff and slow. The sun was coming up the next morning by then. She wasn't bleeding any more but her skinned flesh was thick with flies which she accepted, as she had accepted every trial in her life until now, with meek resignation.

There wasn't much grazing to be had among the sand and

boulders, thistles and cacti, and there was no water at all. By this time her thirst was terrible. She lifted her head high to smell out the direction of a water course, her pink nostrils opening wide to breathe in only dust and heat. Then she lowered it again and, as the day progressed, her head drooped more and more until her muzzle almost dragged along the ground as she plodded homewards, instinctively facing the right direction.

That night she heard the coyote. She trembled as she listened to the rapid, high-pitched yaps flowing into an ecstatic wail. Never before had she been so aware of being alone and, for the first time in her five years, a fear more primitive than anything she had ever experienced stirred deep where the spirit had been beaten and starved out of her as a yearling.

The coyote got the scent of her and began to track her, not

always within her sight but usually within her scent or hearing. Sometimes as she plodded homeward she felt she had escaped him but then his big russet ears and appraising eyes would appear from behind a rock or above a dip in the ground. He knew she was weak with thirst and slowed by her injuries, but he hadn't yet calculated to his own satisfaction just how much of a fight she might put up if he attacked her. The fact that she didn't go for him was very encouraging.

He followed her for several days, filling his empty belly with mice and carrion as he came across it, as much curious about her as eager to taste her flesh. A more spirited animal would have turned on him by this time and chased him off, but the golden palomino accepted his harrying as she accepted everything in her life.

By the fourth day the coyote was reaching the border of his territory. His curiosity was satisfied. As the indifferent sun rose to renew its daily promise of heat and thirst the mare knew as well as he did that this would be the last day of the chase. She set off with flattened ears and tired legs, and whether it was her own nervousness or his slavering decision that drove her first to a trot, then to a canter, neither of them knew. Though trembling with weakness, her legs took charge, driven by the fearful impulse of her heart, and soon they extended to a full gallop, the coyote loping along behind with a grin of satisfaction in the stretch of his jaws. He could have overtaken her sooner but still he was cautious enough to want no fight for his meat. Her flight was all to his favour.

Suddenly, above the pounding of hooves on the hard ground, above the rasp of the mare's choked breath, came a trumpeting squeal that stopped the coyote in his tracks. Charging across the stony, scrub-strewn land in a line that cut directly between hunter and hunted, a small bay stallion, all thick black mane and iron muscles, came snake-like towards the astonished coyote. Ears flat, nostrils wide, threat alone was enough to send the hunter off in the opposite direction, tail between his legs, yelping with fear.

The stallion hardly bothered to follow him, being more interested in the palomino mare who stood with heaving flanks and hanging head, breathing noisily. A whicker of greeting broke from him as slowly he pranced towards her, lifting his black forelegs as high as he could, arching his thick neck as he danced sideways towards her, deep sounds coming from his throat.

He hadn't picked the best moment in which to show off his strength and power. Exhaustion had glazed her vision and reduced her sense of smell and as he circled round her, demanding attention, she didn't even raise her head or move an ear, hardly yet able to realize that the coyote would no longer molest her.

The stallion gave up his display and with much movement of his ears began sniffing her all over. The smell of her injuries alarmed him, making him draw away, but the fact that she was a mare and new to him soon tempted him back. Nostrils close to hers, he wooed her with soft breaths and little encouraging squeals and after a while she began to respond, snorting back at him in a very timid and tentative way.

Since her earliest days she had had almost no contact with others of her kind and this tough little bay stallion, at least a hand shorter than she was, busying himself about her in a not unfriendly way, was entirely beyond her comprehension.

In his turn, the stallion didn't know what to make of her.

The history of her last few days – shock, pain, hunger, thirst, even her acceptance of death – all these things could be sensed by him, repelling and frightening him. He took in her history with an angry, fearsome squeal of protest, throwing up his head and rearing as if to shake off all acknowledgement of it, causing the palomino to shrink in fear of him.

Back on all fours, he stretched forward to sniff at the leather head-collar with its brass rings and lingering smell of polish and human hands which made him squeal and toss again. He even took a nip at her to emphasize his protest, catching her cheek. As she threw back her own head to escape his sudden anger, the noseband hit the stallion under the chin and he jumped away in terror of the man-made thing.

For a few moments he kept at a distance from her, ears working back and forth as he remembered the herd of mares waiting for him over the hill. He always expected rivals to come along in his absence to steal his mares and was aware that he had left them alone for some little time. Habit, combined with protective instinct, urged him to race back to them; but here was this new female, an equally strong temptation.

The palomino helped him to decide. She pricked her ears, lifted her tail and whinnied for him to come back to her, not wanting to be left alone. It was the first spirited action of her life.

3

The desert areas of Chihuahua's isolated tableland, stretched between two vast mountain ranges, had never been intended by nature as a breeding ground for horses. For much of the year the grey and brown earth produced only scanty nibbling, enough for jack rabbits and rodents who kept out of the sun and needed no water. In turn these creatures kept coyotes, bobcats, foxes and buzzards alive. Between April and October it rained and, in the way of desert plants, the agaves and ocotillo, the prickly pear and fuzzy-looking yucca, mesquite, Christmas cactus and all the rest stored up the precious liquid, drop by drop, hallowing it into life for another year.

The ground was always hard and dusty, scattered with the rocks and boulders of some prehistoric upheaval. There was hardly a river, hardly a stream, hardly a lake, although, near the mountains, there were dried-up remnants of the latter where mesquite and tufts of hardy, wire-like grass, grey rather than green, straggled in determined existence.

Harsh, inhospitable, bereft of wooded hills or green plains and valleys, scarred only by jagged ravines in mocking reminder of a time when there had been water and fecundity, this hostile terrain could only be looked upon by any grazing animal as a last retreat.

Such it was for the bay stallion and his kind, true mustangs, descendants of the Spanish horses brought to Mexico by Cortez, which in a hundred generations had filled the wide open spaces with the sounds of their hooves and battle cries, and yet in only a hundred years had been almost totally exterminated. Their lush valleys had become large *haciendas*, their watering places private property, their prairies had been broken for the cultivation of grain. Like the Indians, they had been forcibly driven to desert and mountain in order to survive. Even then, wherever there was man, for the wild horse there was death or captivity.

Faced with extinction, in twos and threes and small family groups the wild horses found refuge in places where man rarely ventured. They had a thousand years of Persian, Arab and Berber blood, together with an inherited memory of barren deserts, windswept plateaus and the bitterly cold highlands of Central Asia to aid them as nature worked its final honing, gave them one last chance.

With bodily necessities reduced to an absolute minimum, gone was the beauty which had first captured the imagination of man; gone was the gentleness which could turn them into slaves. They were small and scraggy, narrow, light of frame, so that they could chase and overtake the wind, but deep in the chest for lungs that had expanded through generations of pursuit. Beneath their hides there was nothing but muscle and bone and their spirits were forged of the very same iron that had kept their small hooves drumming since their first escape into freedom from Cortez's men. For all this, only the very toughest, only the wiliest and strongest-hearted survived.

This was the bay stallion's inheritance, and in the twelve years of his existence he had made use of it well enough to get himself a harem of five mares and keep them alive through summer heat and winter freeze, guarding his territory against intruders with the savage jealousy of any king threatened by invasion.

His boundaries were well defined, his summer range being this land of prickly pear and spiky yucca where, at any moment, the rainy season would begin. Clouds were already gathering. When they burst the parched earth would be slashed into hundreds of washes, hard ground suddenly a quagmire. Red, yellow, orange and green flowers would bloom everywhere while ferocious rain storms turned the dry, shallow basins into lakes which as soon as the rainy season was over would be empty once more, their moisture reabsorbed by the sun.

As winter came on he moved his family into the mountains, leaving behind the hoar-frosted desert nights. There was a valley he knew of at the bottom of a ravine, too inaccessible to have been discovered yet by man but big enough for the requirements of his mares and colts. On the rim of the gorge, a thousand feet above, the snow would be thick, the winds bitter and constant; the narrow tracks of mule-deer and big-horn along which they had come would be completely impassable until the spring melting, when water would come cascading down the rockface to swell the placid, jade-green stream beside which they did their winter grazing. The stream would become a river, with the water rising perhaps twenty feet or more – there were dead branches and drift-wood caught in rock crevices and in the angles between plants growing out of the cliff side to warn how high the water could reach – but before this ever happened the bay stallion would be on his way back to the desert, instinctively knowing when the passes were again open to them.

He always returned to the same place, far away from streams, marshes or rivers where there was always danger, but within a few miles of the only permanent water-hole he knew of, where the territories of several stallions overlapped and where battles had taken place until a drinking order had been established. It was an unreliable water supply, a hole in the ground that in bad years dried out completely, but the only one they had. Only horses that could adapt to heat, cold, thirst and hunger, could survive there.

4

As the bay stallion returned to his herd, pushing the palomino before him, all thirteen members of it simultaneously raised their heads, ears pricked, intensely curious. The palomino halted in her tracks at the sight of them but the stallion urged her forward, anxious to check that all was well, that none was missing. By the time they were close the herd had more or less bunched together, suspicious enough of the stranger to close ranks. When the palomino halted again, sensing the little herd's hostility as well as its curiosity, the bay left her to go forward on his own, blowing and squealing greetings as he circled round and checked them all.

Meanwhile, one of the mares detached herself from the rest and, with a very belligerent expression, ears flattened, nostrils and mouth pursed, came prancing sideways towards the palomino. This was the lead mare, a grey with black points, whose authority in the herd was in many ways higher even than the stallion's. She was extremely jealous of any new herd member and would waste no time in exacting the respect she considered her due.

Too terrified to run, the palomino shrank before her, drawing in her hindquarters and squeezing her tail between her legs in an effort to make herself look small and insignificant. Although she had been afraid of the stallion, she had at least sensed a friendly interest in him, but she was as petrified by this bullying mare as she had been by the coyote; she was overcome by the ill-will exuding from the high prancing legs, arched neck and bared upper incisors. She lowered her head and let her ears flop sideways, cringing in the most abject submission. The grey retaliated by tearing a mouthful of mane from her withers, then contemptuously kicking at her as she turned back to the herd, spitting out bits of hair on the way.

The palomino stayed rooted to the spot with the same submissive expression and fear until each mare in her turn had come to take a look at her, accompanied by their youngsters who, in spite of their youth, followed their mothers' examples and treated her with scorn. Then they forgot about her and went back to their grazing, but over the next few days Don Rafael's mare knew little peace among them. Each one was determined that this newcomer should make no difference to her position in the herd, and so for several days the anxiety caused by her arrival rippled among them, making them as wary and bad-tempered with each other as they were with her.

The stallion had nothing to do with squabbles among his mares so, despite his preliminary interest in her, he cared little that she was nipped by one, buffeted by another, hardly allowed to graze or rest until worry and jealousy were finally appeased and they were sure she knew she was the lowest among them, the last in drinking order, the first to be turned on in a moment of bad temper. Even the two-year-olds and the yearlings, protected by their dams' authority, had more standing in the herd than she did and, although she presented a submissive attitude whenever they came to tease her, their high spirits made them aggressive.

She had lost half her mane and bits of her tail before a week was out but, in spite of this, it never occurred to her to try to escape them. If once she had had the intention of returning home to that good bucket of feed and Don Rafael, that intention was now forgotten. More powerful instincts were at work within her and, after the preliminary hazing, which she

24

endured as she had endured all the hard things of her life so far, she was as much a member of the bay stallion's family as the rest.

She discovered the relationships existing between individual animals. The lead mare had a bay yearling colt, his plain colouring broken by a white blaze that covered most of his head. Although he was always tagging behind the stallion and trying to imitate him, he was still young enough to snatch the occasional mouthful of milk from his dam who, because this year she was barren, still had a negligible supply for him. The rangy two-year-old with dappled hide, black legs and muzzle, was his brother and there was a lot of jealousy between them. Both had inherited their dam's autocratic bearing and although the yearling always came off worse in their quarrels he was always the first to start them.

Another two-year-old colt, a pink sorrel with a brown head, sometimes joined in their battles, but he was usually the scapegoat of the reckless, high-spirited games that all the male youngsters indulged in. His dam, a pink sorrel like himself, had been until the palomino's arrival the most inferior member of the herd and therefore, though older than the rest, the sorrel colt had this disadvantage of his birth. The others knew he was a nobody, he knew he was a nobody and, when the games turned into squabbles, as they often did when they all grew tired or one of them tried to exert his authority and the rest wouldn't let him, they would all turn on the sorrel in their frustration and he would meekly submit to them. As yet he had no stallion instincts at all and the stud completely ignored him, sensing no danger in him. He kept his eye sharply on the others though, and now and again gave them a few punishing nips.

The stallion seemed to have forgotten the palomino and took no notice of her. His favourite was the grey and they often stood together in the afternoon, head to tail, swishing the flies off each other and nibbling at each other's coat. All the mares had grooming companions except the palomino, who stood alone in the afternoon heat and rubbed the itchy, healing places on her back and flank as best she could.

She kept at a good distance from the mares, afraid of their threats even though these were but rarely followed by a bite or a kick. The grey lead mare would sometimes take it into her head to bully the palomino, chasing her with flattened ears and bared teeth. She would attack the others from time to time, too, but only the palomino seemed to bring out the worst in her.

Sometimes the stallion would become restless, perhaps getting wind of a rival stallion or a bobcat, and then he would snake round his mares and drive them into a close-knit band, refusing to let them split up and return to grazing until his mood had passed. The palomino was less frightened of him than she was of the grey and instead of running towards the herd she would head off in an opposite direction, anticipating the punishment the grey would have in store for her just as soon as she was hustled up beside her. She would get bitten and kicked by both of them when eventually brought back, with the others taking advantage of the moment to get in a kick or a nip, too, bad-tempered in the general nervousness that had been aroused.

Towards the end of her second week among them, the pink sorrel mare made tentative efforts at friendship but the palomino responded to these overtures with the same submissive gesture she used when threatened, unable in her fearfulness to recognize the different approach, and the sorrel wandered off again, slightly puzzled.

The main obstruction to the herd's acceptance of her was the head-collar that she didn't even notice. Although it no longer had any human smell about it, it was such a strange object, so much beyond the experience of any of them, that they were instinctively afraid of it and wary of the horse that wore it. It set her apart and was an irritation to them. Although she was now accepted, knew her place and made no attempt to usurp the position of any of them, they didn't like her.

5

After almost no time at all Don Rafael wouldn't have recognized the palomino to which he had devoted so much time, effort and love. Now there was no shine to her coat, which was thick with dust from the daily rollings she indulged in to keep out the heat and deaden the irritating effect of the flies. Her mane was ragged and chewed; the long forelock which had always fallen so gracefully over her eyes stuck up like a brush, thick with burrs, and her tail was equally stiff and cluttered. Her muzzle and lips were full of cuts and scratches, swollen with little fine cactus spines, as she painfully learnt to get the better of prickly pear and thistle, and the slowly healing, fly-ridden mass of scabs which stretched from withers to rump would have made the old man shudder with horror. All her fat had gone and even her flesh seemed to have shrunk, dried out by the heat and shortage of water, but she was at that time probably in as good a shape as any of the bay stallion's band.

This was not to say much for any of them. The sun shone on rib-patterned hides all round and the mares with big bellies were carrying foals, not fat. They were all of a scarecrow appearance, even the stallion, in spite of his thick, proud neck and powerful muscles. All of them were waiting for the rain.

The desert came alive after a rainfall, with even the saddest-looking cactus bursting into bloom. As big black thunderclouds gathered in a sky now only a pale reflection of its former vivid blue, the very earth and all that lived upon it seemed stilled in subdued expectation. The horses stood in a bunch, ears pricked, hardly moving; cicadas were silent and no birds chirped; even the spectral cacti, forever stretching out, poking up or leaning in strange directions, lost their menace before the clouds exploded and the downpour came. It would last perhaps half an hour, rarely more, turning the desert surface into a quagmire, forming lakes in every shallow and, although in two days the ground would be hard and dry and cracked again, in that short time the desert changed its colour. Yellow paper flowers burst into bloom among the stones, chino grama grass sprouted green and strong; there was suddenly a profusion of growing things everywhere amid the pervading scent of creosote from the bushes, and the horses grazed with fierce intensity, all quarrels forgotten as they spread out over a wide area to forage to the best advantage.

At midday, with the sun at its highest, the stallion rounded them up, ever aware of the danger of allowing his mares to stray, and for several hours they dozed in a group, keeping the flies off each other with their bodies and tails.

In the early part of the day, with teeth tearing hurriedly to fill their always hungry bellies, the flies were hardly noticed but as the sun grew high, shadows short and stomachs fuller, the herd began to feel them. Heads tossed, legs stamped, tails swished, skins trembled. The movement was almost constant and yet unavailing. Expressions were irked and tempers short but the flies blithely continued to suck moisture from the corners of their eyes, scavenge all over the most sensitive parts of their bodies, clean themselves, bask in the sun and start all over again. These flies, gathering with plague-like intensity, urged the horses to higher ground, to fresh breezes and cool tree shades. The eastern slopes of the *cordillera* were temptingly dotted with Douglas firs, oaks and *madrones*, whose rhododendron-like leaves offered plenty of shade, but they were some ten miles from the water-hole and had no streams, springs or seeps. However, such were the temptations of the high ground that the whole herd trekked there and back daily, grazing in that direction from sunrise onwards so that by midday they were under the trees, out of the sun and away from the flies. Over the years all of them had developed a long, mile-eating stride, and by nightfall they were back at the water-hole again, hardly wearied by the trek.

Such a routine was hard on the palomino, still struggling to adapt herself to so sparse an existence, and she would have fallen far behind, or perhaps not even have followed them, had not the stallion, who kept wary eyes on every herd member, urged her on with angry squeals and bites. He cared nothing for her lameness when an agave spine pierced her fetlock; he paid no heed to her weariness; and because he was more dreadful to her than pain and weariness together, she obeyed him and kept up with the rest.

The stallion was now at his most alert and aggressive, for the rainy season also marked the time for the mares carrying foals to give birth and the barren ones to come into season. There were several lone studs, some of them sons of his own, grazing neighbouring terrains. Their paths often crossed his and they were only too eager to steal either a mare or the whole harem from him just as soon as the breeze carried a mating scent to them.

He kept the mares under the tightest surveillance, hazing round them, chasing them into a close bunch whenever they were too scattered for his liking. Night and day his vigilance never faltered. He grazed only in snatches, raising his head between each mouthful, his little ears working in every direction, his dark eyes taking in every shadow, every moving leaf. Nothing escaped his attention, not even when he was engaged in love-play with his favourite mare.

He drove both the grey's colts out of the herd that summer,

first Black Legs who was paying far too much attention to the palomino and a striped dun mare who was also barren. Black Legs didn't take his banishment seriously at first, sneaking back at dusk, wanting the company of the herd, but the stallion drove at him with a fury beyond anything he had ever shown before, ripping a chunk from his rump with a killer's expression in his flattened ears. Black Legs was terrified and didn't stop running until there were several miles between himself and his sire. Now and again he ventured as far as the borders of the stallion's territory but was too afraid to come to drink at the water-hole until several days had passed and thirst got the better of fear. Meanwhile he met up with his brother, the white-blazed yearling, who had also aroused the stallion's animosity, and the two outlaws roamed the edges of their father's range together, sometimes whinnying plaintively towards their lost companions while warily watching for any move on the stallion's part to drive them off again.

The white-patched dun, the pink sorrel and the buckskin mare produced foals one after the other and the lead mare was jealous of each in turn because she had no foal of her own. As each youngster was brought into the herd, a couple of days old and ready to be introduced, she tried to steal it for herself, using her meanest tactics to drive the mother away. But even the pink sorrel was having none of that, motherhood increasing her stature in the herd. The grey found her subordinates retaliating with unusual spirit and, in the most malicious of moods, vented her frustration on the palomino.

She followed her everywhere, ears set balefully, upper incisors showing, neither grazing herself nor allowing her victim to graze as she hounded her from place to place. Her malevolence alone was enough to destroy the palomino's very insecure sense of contentment. It wasn't necessary for her actually to use her teeth or hooves.

Whenever the grey came into sight the palomino moved off. But for the bay stallion's constant vigilance she would have been driven right off his range and into the company of the only too eager Black Legs and White Blaze. When they strayed too far he would come squealing after both of them, his lowered head weaving from side to side in threatening, snake-like motion. This was enough to send the grey obediently back to the others but the palomino, her nerves in rags, would stand and wait for him with trembling legs, then dash off blindly in any direction to escape the bites she knew were coming to her. As soon as she was back with the herd the grey would be after her again, and so it went on until her enemy's frustration at having no foal at foot had passed.

There was little peace for any of them in summer. Now and again a stallion would come to challenge the bay and, before turning to face him, he would send all the mares galloping to a safe distance under the protection of the grey. On his return from the challenge, which sometimes consisted only of a show of bravado, but now and then developed into a scuffle, he would chase his mares back and forth in circles as if determined to keep them in good shape for the next time, or perhaps just to confirm to them that he was still boss. None of the challenging stallions stood up to him for long. He had the advantage of being on his own territory and, at twelve years, sufficient maturity and self-confidence to intimidate most enemies by a display of strength alone.

Even when he occasionally ventured into a neighbouring stallion's territory, the chances were that his neighbour would remove his harem to a discreet distance, with just a warning in his snorts that he would only tolerate so much, and the bay stallion would move back in his own good time. He made no effort to steal his neighbours' mares, well satisfied with his own band which was about as much as he could handle with confidence.

In fact, before the summer was over, he allowed a young black stud to go off with his two-year-old fillies with only a token show of protest. The black was a five-year-old who had been roaming the territory as a loner for some time, looking for a chance to gather a harem of his own. The two fillies had no desire to go off with him and both fled from his inexperienced herding, doubling back to the band they belonged to. He chased after them but skidded to an uncertain halt as the bay stallion came prancing forward to see what he was up to.

Now the bay didn't like his own daughters because when they came into their first season they attracted so many suitors that the unity of the whole herd was threatened. Even he couldn't fight off five or six stallions in one day and still keep his family intact so, when he saw the fillies galloping back, and the black stallion not knowing what to do about it, he chased them off himself, much to their bewilderment for they had looked to him for protection. The black took up the pursuit again when the two fillies were once more within reach of him and this time he kept them running in the right direction, away from their dams.

Two colts and a filly were born to the mares that summer and they chased each other over the hard desert ground whenever they weren't suckling or sleeping. The palomino watched them with curiosity but kept well away from them, nervous of their high spirits. She and the pink sorrel mare were on friendlier terms now and often grazed fairly close to each other, but whenever the sorrel's little filly foal came gambolling up for a feed she quickly moved out of the way, ears laid back in fear of her. She sensed the sudden protective instinct that overcame the mother just as soon as her offspring approached and anticipated some kind of rebuff.

At times she was tempted to sniff noses with the foal but at the last moment courage failed her. Once when she and the sorrel were grazing side by side the filly foal tried to suckle her by mistake. She shot up in the air as if discovering a rattler among the stones and for two days after that kept a very wary eye on her companion's offspring. As yet, she had no mothering instincts of her own.

6

The rainy season ended in October and very soon after that it looked as though water never fell in the desert at all. The basins were dry again, with no vestige of ever having contained water, and the stony ground was cracked, crazy-quilt fashion, with some of the cracks up to ten feet wide. The cacti bristled starkly, all their life in roots deep under the earth. There were no flowers now and the wind blew sand fiercely into the horses' eyes and nostrils, causing them to turn their backs and huddle against it.

Dawn was often frost grey and the mares stood around with drooping ears and tight tails, miserable with cold. The stallion would rouse them, making them rush frantically in wide circles to stir their blood. His craze for herding them these cold mornings kept them alert and together at a time when any mare or youngster, misjudging its distance from the herd in a fog or a sandstorm, could fall easy prey to a marauding pack of coyotes or a hungry bobcat.

Black Legs and White Blaze tried to rejoin the herd, their high summer spirits subdued by the change in the weather but, although the bay stallion was having none of this, he did not resent the sight of them at a distance. Very tentatively did they try to reduce the indefinable limit he had set on their approach and each day saw them a little closer.

One morning White Blaze forgot all caution as the grey mare caught sight of him and whinnied longingly to him. He flung himself forward, eagerly answering, but before half the distance was covered between the two animals, mother and son, the bay stallion was thrusting down upon them like a whirlwind. Black Legs, though not the culprit this time, saw him coming first and took flight, but his brother left it too late.

Bodies collided, shoulder to shoulder, and White Blaze crumpled up under the crash. Too terrified even to try scrambling to all fours again, he allowed the stallion to stand over him and pull chunks of hair from his mane. His immediate anger satisfied, the stallion then allowed him to get up, and poor White Blaze, thoroughly crushed, returned to the instincts of his foalhood for defence, making suckling noises and chewing movements with his lips. This worked better than he could have hoped, for after thoroughly chastising him, instead of driving him off, the stallion relented and pushed him back into the herd.

After that Black Legs had to run alone. There was no relenting of his father's rule for him.

In the way that animals have, all the herd knew that it was time to move to their wintering ground. More and more often now in the afternoon dozing period did they turn their heads towards the sierra, and the general restlessness became first a longing and then a definite intention to move. All they waited for was for the grey mare to take the lead. Until she did so not even the stallion would try to drive them.

At last, one evening they began to move, shortly after they had drunk their fill at the desert watering hole, the palomino only approaching long after all the rest had finished. The whole desert was a blaze of orange and red from the westering sun and it was in the direction of the sun that the lead mare eventually turned with a long, determined and yet easy stride, the rest falling in behind her.

The palomino was still mouthing the water at the hole when they set out, loath to leave it, less able to withstand the long periods without water which the others took for granted.

Watching and listening to them all drinking while she timidly waited her turn was a torment only endurable because, when the last one had gone away, she could take over and stand there for as long as she liked, dribbling the cool liquid through her jaws, blowing into it, almost caressing it. She became part of the sky's golden glow as she lifted her head curiously to watch them, with no urge to follow. Usually they began the night's foraging at this time but there was no sign of that.

They were strung out in a line, in twos and threes, small units of mothers and sons and daughters together, and if there was a certain sense of urgency in their pace it was because they knew from other occasions that there would be no more water for them until they reached the mountains.

The palomino didn't know what to do, tempted to stay by the water but anxious as the distance between herself and the herd grew. The stallion was the last in the line and so far hadn't missed her. It wasn't until one of his colts, a yearling buckskin, took it into his head to play stallion himself, usurping the all-important last in the line position – prancing along as if he were driving the whole herd before him, including his sire – that the bay stallion, turning round on him in immense irritation, caught a glimpse of the palomino still standing beside the water-hole. First things first, however.

He flung himself at the buckskin colt and ripped a mouthful of mane from his withers before chasing him up to a position just behind his dam, and then he cantered back to the water-hole with a bad-tempered thrust in his movements which had the palomino trembling before he reached her.

As usual she fled away both from him and the herd, panic-stricken by the stallion's squeal of annoyance. She swung round in a circle, instinctively unwilling to lose sight of the herd altogether, drawn by its magnetic hold over her, and the stallion cut across to keep her headed in the right direction. She swerved to avoid him, ears drawn back as she went away again, and he skidded to a halt almost on the spot, changing direction to cut her off once more. His shoulder crashed against hers, knocking her sideways. As she struggled to all fours again the stallion bit her rump, squealing dire threats as he shouldered her forward towards the herd.

This time she obeyed, eyes wild with fear, but to her surprise when she caught up with the band at an unbalanced, ungainly half trot, half lope, the lead mare didn't swing round to punish her. She slipped into place behind the pink sorrel and her young, sweating and trembling, but glad in her way to be where she belonged, although she didn't have sense enough to get there on her own.

The little herd trekked on for most of the night, the desert bright beneath a full moon in a cloudless sky, weird cactus shapes silhouetted among the rocks and bushes. Before the sun rose they dozed, youngsters sprawled over the ground, the mares standing guard over them, eyes closed but ears alert. After grazing for a while at dawn they went on again, the colts and fillies kicking and bucking in high spirits and the buckskin trying once more to take over his father's role, this time flanking the column as it moved ahead, trying to impress the mares by arching his neck and lifting high his legs, blowing through his nostrils in a commanding way. When the stallion came charging up to him he dashed right through the mares to escape, forgetting his pride, and was scared enough for a few hours to stay in line behind his dam.

The memory of the next watering place kept the mares going at a steady pace all morning, heads lowered and eyes closed against biting winds. The buckskin lost his desire to play stallion, the foals no longer skipped. It was a silent, energy-conserving herd that climbed upwards and on. In places the ground was covered with sharp rocks through which they had to pick their way carefully. At times their pathway bordered on a precipice that fell away to waterfalls and rivers in narrow gorges hundreds of feet below. Cacti clung to the rock face and grew in different varieties along narrow ledges; the white sinuous roots of wild fig trees meandered like frozen water among the fissures; blue butterflies hovered over flowering bushes.

When they reached the rim of the canyon they came to a thin, shallow stream where they all drank long and slowly before splashing onwards, following its stony bed down into the gorge. Their stride became shorter and slower because soon the side of the cliff was almost sheer, easy enough for the big-horn to scamper over but hard going for the horses who had to place one hoof very carefully in front of the other. One of the foals tumbled down a long stretch but, though badly shaken, was none the worse for his experience. He was very careful after that. They passed shallow caves, acacia trees, rocks green with moss and stained in long black streaks where water seeped out of crevices, and at last they came to a sandy beach beside the river. Here at least there was no lack of water.

It was midday and, true to their habits, they stopped to rest and doze, though their bellies were empty. The foals slept deeply and even the yearlings lay down for a while, weary after so strenuous a descent. But still they hadn't reached their destination.

A dozen times that afternoon they crossed and recrossed the river, fording it whenever a wall of blank rock brought the trail to an abrupt end. The palomino balked at plunging her hooves into that ice-cold water – she had never done such a thing in her life – but the stallion forced her on, his bay coat turned almost to black as he splashed back and forth. The foals squealed and thrashed about but followed closely beside their dams, both frightened and excited by this new experience. The light was going when they began climbing away from the river to pass through a cleft in what looked like impenetrable rock. Bats made shadows in the darkening sky, making the horses toss their heads nervously in spite of their near exhaustion. However, their journey was almost over and the mares all knew it, quickening their pace, pricking their ears, whickering encouragingly to the youngsters.

Suddenly the rocks ended and they were hock high in grass that hadn't been grazed since the previous winter. Ahead the grass gave way to reeds, six feet high and winter brown, bordering a small green pool in which a pair of red-headed ducks paddled tranquilly. Wild kapok trees grew amidst the acacia, cactus and agave beyond the pool, and all along this narrow valley, green with grass, green with water as far as the horses could see, the cliffs towered high and overwhelmingly, protecting it from the cold, fog and wind to be found a thousand feet above.

The ducks flew off with squawks of warning and surprise as the horses approached and there was much flapping and splashing among the reeds as birds which were settling for the night were roughly awakened by a trembling of earth under anxious hooves. But silence quickly returned as the mares stretched out along the grassy bank both to drink and graze, a silence interspersed by a snort or a whicker, sounds that were to be heard often over the next few months.

The palomino hung back as she always did, waiting for them all to go away before daring to come forward for her share of the water. She had to wait a long time because every animal immediately dropped its head to graze, hardly needing to move because the grass was so abundant. At last she came forward, when the youngsters were stretched out among the shadows in the usual abandoned fashion, the mares not far from them, and the stallion pranced with alert ears and wide nostrils at a distance, checking on any changes in his valley since the previous year.

Gratefully she came to drink. The water was ice cold, savouring of the many minerals in the rocks through which it had seeped year after year for thousands of years. She sucked it up slowly in long, steady draughts, feeling the weariness within her drift away, and then she too turned to the grass that reached higher than her fetlocks along the bank, tearing at it as if her starved frame could never get its fill.

The stallion was the last to graze. With the greatest of care did he cover the whole of his winter territory; testing the wind, identifying each scent it carried; snorting at a broken trunk which hadn't lain there before; marking his borders with dung to remind any usurper that he was back, reclaiming what was his; finding nothing to disturb him. Thus it had always been. He pranced through a scattered bunch of mule-deer whose big, bright eyes had been curiously watching him. They often grazed alongside the horses, aware that the stallion was always on guard, ready to signal his distrust of the slightest unusual sign. Cougars lived and hunted in the canyon. Normally they kept well away from the bay stallion's band but they could be tempted close by a straying youngster or a weak mare. Sometimes the cougar scent was in the air or in the grass among the kapok trees. Apart from this they had no enemies in this two furlong stretch of grass and water, not even hunger or cold.

They would stay until the constant surging of the nearby river became a threatening noise instead of harmonic sound, and until all the grazing was exhausted. Only then would it be time to look to the desert for sustenance, before the whole valley was flooded and dangerous and the water became an enemy. Meanwhile the foals grew tall and strong and learnt that there were other things in life beside their mothers' milk, and the mares filled their bellies with lush grass against the time when it would be only a memory.

Thus the palomino spent her first year of freedom in the desert and mountain, with nature working constantly on her body to adapt her to all the extremes she might have to face: long periods without water, constant hunger or a surfeit of grazing, heat and cold. She was much taller than her companions and suffered because of it, being gaunt in the extreme for most of the year. Her very nature kept her thin because she covered more ground than any of them, avoiding the mares and being brought back by the stallion. She looked as wild now as any of the mustangs, a taut ball of nervous energy ready to flee at the slightest pretext, and but for the head-collar would have been unrecognizable as a once domesticated animal.

Don Rafael had sent her across the desert to be got in foal by a quarter-horse stallion of renown, golden and pampered as she was, but when she returned for the second time it was the foal of a little mustang, as prickly and enduring as the desert cactus, that she carried within her.

Foalhood

I

In the palomino's second summer with the herd, the grey lead mare was the first to give birth. Three days after the start of the first heavy rains she went off on her own and hardly twenty-four hours later the palomino was following her example, except that for her it was the first time and she knew nothing of foaling.

She separated herself as far from the herd as she dared, compelled by an instinct much stronger than her fear of the stallion's wrath, not following them when they began their evening trek back to the desert water-hole after spending the afternoon dozing under the trees on their favourite slope. For some time she just stood watching their retreat then, all of a sudden, she turned to climb to the very top of this hump-backed ridge. Here she paused for a while to survey the vista of dense *manzanita* shrubs, pines and oak, the ground rocky and hard, seeking a place of safety with nervous eyes and flared nostrils.

Bulging flanks accentuated her extreme emaciation. It had been a hard year for the palomino with the foal sapping most of her strength and, although she was on the point of giving birth, the udder that should have been full and ready held little promise for a fresh-dropped foal. As she stood wearily on the ridge, she turned her head to look at her flank as if wondering at the strong pangs she was experiencing. She wanted to lie down and give in to them but stronger still was the need to find a safer, more secluded stopping place.

Anxious as always, doubly afraid because she was alone, yet needing very much to be alone, she moved on once more, her flattened ears expressing the urgency of the pains within her. It was hard to keep up her pace and ignore them.

Her chest and neck were soaked with sweat, her face was thin with tiredness by the time she found what she was looking for – a shallow basin surrounded by shrubs and overshadowed by the tall, straight trunk of a solitary fir tree to whose withered, dying branches clung only a remnant of its former foliage – the colour of the earth. The ground was blanketed with dead needles and the palomino sniffed cautiously to discover if any creature had been here before her. There was nothing to make her afraid, though she looked round very carefully before at long last allowing her pain-racked body to collapse. With a groan she rolled on to her flank and stretched out her neck, giving in to the foal's ever stronger demands to be born.

She got up and lay down again several times because the foal was as tired as she was and took long in coming, so that she hardly knew what to do with herself. A pair of black hooves and a black nose were eventually thrust into the sunlight and then, with a rush, the rest of the lanky body tumbled to the ground to begin its struggle for independence, for air, for life. Now his head was free of the sac that had sheltered him since his first moment of being and his little mouth opened in his first half bleat, half gasp of protest at the pain of being born.

The palomino was too jaded by her own efforts to be aware of his struggle or his cry. While he rolled and weaved to free himself of the membrane still holding him prisoner she lay unmoving, her eyes closed against the sun which had changed position all this while and taken away the shade. Now it gleamed on the foal's dark, wet head and floppy ears, on the palomino's spent and sweated frame, and its warmth gave encouragement to them both.

At the foal's second bleat, forced out of him by a frustrated attempt to do something with the legs crumpled up under him, the palomino seemed to wake up. She pricked her ears and scrambled to all fours but when she saw and smelled the foal she jumped away with a snort of fearful astonishment, not knowing what to make of him. For a few seconds they stared at each other, the mare ready to shy off, the foal half sitting with front legs stuck out stiffly, less aware of his dam than of the problem of sorting himself out.

Now the palomino recognized him as a foal but she still didn't understand that he belonged to her. She remembered her fear of last year's foals, when the mares had threatened her for just so much as sniffing at them, and only lassitude and her inability to make head or tail of this curious situation kept her from putting a distance between herself and him.

A tremendous push almost brought the foal to all fours, though his legs bent and wobbled in every direction, and a second movement intended to straighten them out landed him flat on his back, making the palomino start. Then, with hardly a moment to regain his breath, he was trying again, dumbly aware that there was no life for him until he could co-ordinate these limbs that seemed to have a will of their own, contrary to his.

Two, three, four times he tried and fell, ears flopping everywhere – he hadn't had time yet to discover his ears – but at the fifth attempt his hunger was such that will-power rather than balance kept him standing there, very wobbly and very uncertain as to what he should do next. All this time the palomino made no effort to help him and was only interested in his movements in so far as they might represent a threat to herself. Dried pine needles stuck to his uncleaned skin, flies already crawled about him, but she was moved by no instinct to care for him.

To the foal nothing mattered beyond his need for sustenance. Although he couldn't yet distinguish one end of the palomino's body from the other, instinct took him towards her with movements that alternated between caution and bounce. Whenever he blundered into her, making sucking noises with his curled up tongue, she jumped out of his way. He fell over and got up again half a dozen times, jerkily pursuing her, tongue working desperately.

His bullying blundering, punctuated by irritated bleats, quite intimidated the palomino. She realized that he wanted something of her and eventually, because she was so exhausted and because she was submissive by nature, she gave in to him and stood still. The foal's stiff brush of a tail worked up and down with intense excitement at her surrender even though his search still wasn't over. He pushed and nuzzled at the palomino's bony breast with ever increasing frustration, bleating with anger, stamping a hoof which was now enough under his control to be stamped, and with the indomitable mustang will that was already in him he went on searching.

He worked his hungry black lips and aching tongue along the palomino's belly until, more by accident than judgement, he found a teat in his mouth which responded to his need. Even then the milk didn't flow at once. He had to work very hard to get it and twice the pain it gave to the palomino made her involuntarily kick him away. With blunt determination he was back again within seconds, bleating desperately until at long last the milk began to flow. And then, as he suckled, a change came over the palomino. Anchored to her, greedily dragging out her very life as it seemed, the foal's needs became her own.

She started to nibble at the dirt on his withers and rump and the more she nuzzled and licked the better the milk flowed, the more the colt became one with her. He suckled noisily until there was no longer a hollow pain in his belly. Then the legs he had worked so hard to command seemed to

melt away and he with them. He slipped to the ground, eyes closed, and while he slept the palomino went on nuzzling and nibbling at his head and neck and underparts, whickering softly over him.

2

For two nights the palomino stayed beneath the fir tree amid the *manzanita* bushes with her blackfaced colt. It wasn't a very satisfactory period for either of them for the foal was constantly hungry, dividing his time between desperate suckling and short, exhausted naps. The palomino had so little milk that he was never satisfied and his famished stomach interrupted all his slumbers so that, although he did nothing but suckle and sleep, he was perpetually hungry and tired.

Now the folly of being so far from water became apparent to the palomino. She would prick her ears in its direction, her whole body aching for want of it, but even she could understand that the foal was too weak to travel so far. In spite of her need she was too anxious for his safety to leave him alone, and because there was no water her already drained body could respond no further. All that she ate in those two days, however little, became milk for the foal and she was like a skeleton draped with brittle skin. The head-collar, stiff now and beginning to crack, looked enormous on her.

In the end, despite her anxiety, she had no alternative but to trek back to the water-hole. That, or perish with her colt under the tree. The foal was hardly in a better condition than she was, his dark hide and yellow hair dry and lustreless, his flanks hollow, but there was still some bounce in him as he began to follow her, ears pricked, tail high.

Before they reached the hump-backed ridge the bounce was gone. His fetlocks were still weak, weaker than they might have been had he been able to nurse to greater advantage, and the rocky ground, tangled with uncovered roots and trailing branches, was difficult terrain for him. Only too soon the palomino was having to stop constantly to wait for him to catch up, whickering encouragement in which he could detect a note of urgency. Now and again she pushed him along with her head but this way of travelling was both slow and dangerous because, while occupied with him, she was unable to keep her eyes alert for any threatening signs.

When at last they reached the ridge she gave in to his need to suckle and sleep, regardless of herself. She stayed on the ridge for a couple of hours, the hard journey making the foal sleep longer than was his custom, and when he woke she allowed him to suckle once more, though what little he dragged from her caused her great discomfort.

Hardly had they started down the slope together when the palomino came to an abrupt halt. Just ahead and coming towards her with that wicked expression she knew only too well was the stallion's favourite mare, the grey who had foaled only three days previously not far away. There was about her an intense and desperate air which the palomino immediately sensed without knowing the cause and, although only a few days earlier she would have fled at the sight of her, now she was chained to her colt. She froze to the spot, already trembling. Little Blackface sensed her fear and froze too, both of them staring at the grey who charged straight towards them. At the last minute she swerved to make a complete circle round them, swinging her head low in stallion-like gestures to intimidate her captives to the maximum. As she circled milk streamed from her swollen udder and Blackface, who was more bewildered than frightened, caught the scent of it and uttered a loud, shrill cry of hunger. This brought the grey mare to an immediate standstill.

Some twenty-four hours earlier she had lost her own foal to a cougar. She had left it for a very short time, asleep in a hidden place, unaware of the cougar that had been stalking her downwind for most of the morning. When she came back the foal was gone and the scent of the cougar was strong in the place where she had left it. She had followed the trail, desperation for her foal overcoming her fear of the cougar, giving out loud whinnies but getting no response.

The grey's maternal instinct was strong and violent. All day and all night she had covered and recovered the ground, the growing discomfort of her full udder adding to her general distress. She was still looking for her youngling, roaming far from where she had lost its trail, when the palomino appeared with Blackface and now, hearing his hungry cry, it took only a few seconds for her to react. The decision was made. She flew straight at the mother, teeth viciously bared, and hardly had the palomino veered away from the attack before she rounded on the foal and pushed him towards her dripping udder.

After his long hours of unceasing hunger Blackface hardly knew how to manage the overfull milk bag that was so generously presented to him. Until now he had had to drag out every swallow, with his tongue getting weary long before his stomach ever got full, and suddenly the milk was choking down his throat without any effort on his part at all. From the spare teat it dripped into his eyes and ran down his neck and, while he guzzled as fast as he could, milk bubbling from the corners of his mouth and even blocking his nostrils, the grey mare belligerently glared at his dam, defying her to come close.

Never had the palomino's distress been so great. The grey was stealing the colt from under her very nose and she didn't know what to do about it. She didn't have the courage to attack her and, even had this not been the case, she wouldn't have had the strength to win any battle of wills. She knew this even better than did the grey, whose whole expression showed how ready she was to fight for the colt's possession.

All she could do was call desperately to her youngling, hoping he would return to her of his own accord.

But Blackface was deaf and blind and dull with a surfeit of milk. At last he staggered away from the grey and collapsed in a heap beside her. She moved to stand guard over him, her front hooves almost touching him, the shadow of her head falling across his unconscious body, and for a couple of hours the three of them didn't move, the palomino with her eyes on the colt, the grey defiantly watching her, while Blackface slept on, oblivious of both.

3

Blackface had been alone with the palomino long enough for him to recognize her as his mother so, as soon as he woke up from his first really long and satisfied slumber, he immediately frolicked to greet her, paying no attention whatsoever to the grey. So intimidated was the palomino by the lead mare that, although she was glad to have him back, as she nibbled at him and blew over him she kept one wary eye on the grey, expecting to have the foal stolen away from her again at any minute. She was afraid, as if she were the intruder, the kidnapper, and yet her motherly instinct kept her from altogether yielding her natural right to him. She offered him her own udder but he was still satiated from his previous gluttony and only briefly nuzzled her sore and dried-up teats.

Meanwhile the grey watched their exchange of greetings and affection without making any move. The colt escaped his mother's attentions and began to try out his legs. It was marvellous how much energy that one good feed had given him. He cantered a complete circle round his mother, totally unbalanced and almost falling over himself, then rushed towards her with butting head, wanting her to join him in the game. She, however, was far too worried to make any sense of his demand and again tried to get him to suckle from her, as if wanting to reassure herself of her right to him. This was when the grey suddenly acted, catapulting forward with bared teeth and threatening squeal.

The palomino fled, with no thought for her foal, but stopped only a hundred yards off, ears pricked longingly while Blackface, after a moment's stiff-legged bewilderment, began to suckle the grey. He sucked for only a couple of minutes, not really hungry but tired already from his game. Soon he was asleep again but this time, instead of standing guard over him, the grey began to graze, wandering quite a little way from him in her search for particular grasses.

Cautiously the palomino got closer, ready for flight but desperate enough to refuse to be driven off altogether. The grey lifted her head and watched her, flattening and pricking her ears until the palomino stood still again, and then she went back to grazing. Little by little the palomino came within ten yards of the sleeping foal but closer than this she dared not move. She could smell him, see him but not touch him, and as long as she moved no closer the grey was prepared to ignore her. Hunger eventually overcame the palomino and she too began to graze. Both mares kept within the sleeping foal's perimeter and, although it might have seemed there was a truce between them, each knew exactly what the position was. Only Blackface was unaware of the unequal tug-of-war.

The next time he woke the grey was already moving towards him, the palomino backing off as she came up but finding the courage to call to her youngling, with just the slightest touch of defiance in her tone for the usurper. Blackface was hungry now. He heard the palomino's whinny but the grey was uttering encouraging little sounds too and she was much nearer. He was obviously confused, his gaze going from one to the other. To his infant eyes and memory they were similar in colouring in the half shadow, half sunlight of the afternoon and he no longer knew which was his dam. Panic struck him, sounding shrill and loud in the cry that burst from him. His mother made to come to his rescue but already the grey was between them, swinging her hindquarters menacingly at the palomino while reaching consolingly for the colt.

Again the palomino had to stand by and watch her foal glut himself from the other mare. She trotted back and forth, whinnying distressfully but not daring to challenge the grey's rights to him, and this time, when he had finished suckling, Blackface had obviously accepted the grey mare as his dam. He frolicked round her, came back to her two or three times for a nuzzling and the odd little pull at her teats, and when he happened to notice the palomino still watching him from a safe distance he stared back with detached curiosity.

That same afternoon the lead mare decided to return to the herd, having fully established to her own satisfaction her right to the palomino's foal and his acceptance of her. When she set off towards the place where the band usually congregated Blackface followed her, his attention caught first by one thing and then another, a swooping bird, a scuttling lizard, the breeze passing noisily through the leaves above his head.

Behind them both, at a suitable distance, came the palomino, still whickering hopefully from time to time but getting no reply. Whenever the grey stopped to look back at her, she stopped too, but she doggedly followed them, not knowing what else to do.

There was a lot of snorting, whickering and nervous moving about among the mares when the grey came back to them, the blackfaced colt almost tethered to her side in fear, eyes boggling at so many of his own kind. Very imperiously did his adoptive mother allow each mare to approach, her ears laid back and hooves and teeth at the ready. The foal stood among them, making submissive sucking gestures with his mouth, but his ears pricked inquisitively as if he already understood that he had no real cause to be afraid of any of them. The palomino stopped at a distance, watching everything.

The bay stallion came forward to make his own investigations when the mares had finished. He smelt the foal thoroughly, discovered his sex, and when the grey decided he had sniffed enough she squealed a warning at him. Then he turned to welcoming her, rubbing his face against hers, gently nipping her withers, snorting and blowing his pleasure. But the grey was only half interested in the stallion and soon sent him off with a squeal and a kick. Seeing the palomino still watching her from a distance, she started at a fast trot towards her with a malicious air, but the stallion anticipated her action and completed it for her, driving the palomino off with flattened tail and a squeal of fear.

For another twenty-four hours the palomino hung about Blackface and the grey mare, watching, waiting hopelessly, backing off in fright whenever the grey so much as swung her head at her, and all this time Blackface didn't even notice her. Back near the water-hole, she began to graze in earnest, her once beautiful body wasted away to nothing and desperately in need of sustenance, and before the colt was a week old she had completely forgotten that once he had been hers.

4

Blackface was to be the handsomest of all the bay stallion's sons. No doubt this was due to the palomino's breeding which, in spite of her poor condition, came through true in her son. She didn't pass on to him the magnificent golden sheen that had once caught Don Rafael's eye – for his skin was as black as a starless night, giving dark undertones to his oatmeal coloured coat – but she gave him her height, her long fine neck, high, strong quarters and deep body. He was taller than any foal ever born in the herd which meant that in order to suckle the grey successfully he had to twist his head and neck in an uncomfortable manner. This was but a minor problem, however, and the grey mare, who had mothered half a dozen foals already, was very patient with this colt almost as tall as she was. Apart from his superior conformation, he was a hundred percent mustang, and in the hard land that was his heritage this was the most that nature could do for him. Whatever might become of him depended entirely upon his own character and circumstances.

In both these respects he was luckier than his dam. The palomino had been born gentle by nature and was easy prey to the ignorant Indian who had broken her spirit and almost her body. From the very beginning there was nothing gentle in Blackface. Had there been, he might well have succumbed in his very first hours when he had had to struggle so hard for what little his mother could give him. He was pushy and arrogant, with the seeds of despotism already there, before the lead mare made him her own and so gave him the favoured position in the herd, above any of the colts or fillies born that summer, above their dams. Only the stallion and his foster mother were superior to him in the herd hierarchy. Even White Blaze, despite his seniority, gave way to him when he came prancing along beside the grey, already making fierce thrusting movements with his head and trying hard to make stallion snorts.

Like all the foals, however, he had a lot to learn. In his first few weeks, before he really became aware of the herd as a unit and his place somewhere at the head of that unit, his hours were divided almost equally between playing, eating and sleeping. He had three other foals to play with but he soon singled out the pinto colt as his special companion. The other two were filly foals, more interested in practising grooming behaviour than dashing wildly about. As soon as either Blackface or the pinto started butting and squealing, they would flee for the protection of their dams and that was the end of the game.

He and the pinto became inseparable during their waking hours, for their high spirits matched pretty equally. The pinto was the son of White Patch and his colouring was similar to hers except that where she was mostly mottled yellow with white patches, he was mostly white with yellow patches. His dam held the second highest position among the mares so that in social standing the two colts were about equal.

From games of catch, when they took it in turn to chase each other, the catcher trying to bite the other's neck or withers, they advanced to practising awkward semi-rears, thrusting their forelegs at each other, all the time their pricked ears and eager expressions belying their intentions, reminding each other that it was only a game which could be broken off at any time by either partner without loss of face. But, as they matured, their infant tussles became more and more contests of will, each determined to make the other accept the inferior position. It was impossible for two horses to maintain equality in the herd. Eventually one would have to give way. But in their first summer both colts were a long way from caring too much about individual superiority and either one would back down or break off a sparring match, because he was tired, because his mother thought he was too far away and was whinnying for his immediate return, or because he suddenly felt hungry. As yet, each returned to his own dam for grooming. Unlike the filly foals, their feelings for each other were expressed in scuffles and chases, not in skin care and skittish squeals.

Blackface's lessons came one after the other. His first thunderstorm terrified him but the lively feel of the air when it was over soon made him forget his fear and sent him prancing in search of adventure again. He squelched through the soggy sand, wondering at the sudden heaviness of his hooves, and explored the taste of wet rock with his ever curious tongue. A rattlesnake's warning almost made his heart stop, and instinct overcame curiosity for once, automatically making him bound backwards. By the time he had recovered, the snake had slipped out of sight. The usually staid mares were spooky and bad tempered, wary of the foals, jealous for the stallion's attentions, and the stallion himself was a large and terrifying presence in the young foal's life. Now was when he was most among his mares, doubly vigilant and zealous, his voice often heard in challenge or command as he warded off outside intruders, watched his growing sons and courted the females that came into season one after the other and even at the same time.

Blackface watched White Blaze and the buckskin practising stallion poses and trying to seduce the mares whenever their sire was otherwise engaged. Most of the mares treated their attempts at wooing with scorn, too accustomed to their juvenile tricks over the last couple of years to take them seriously. White Blaze had lost some of his self-confidence after his humiliating experience the previous year, but the buckskin's determination to usurp his slightly superior position brought back his old spirit and the two of them, when not tussling with each other – sometimes quite viciously – were between them trying to run off with any mare or filly that didn't put up too much resistance. Blackface watched their shows of bluff, their sudden attacks and retreats, their exuberant advances, which were more likely to earn them a kick than a returned caress, and later he would prance off to find the pinto, trying to arch his neck the same way, full of aggressive vigour. He went around with his black brush of a tail held almost constantly on high because every other minute he was ready to spring into action, either to throw himself into a game or to dash away from the older colts.

On one occasion the buckskin gave him a terrible fright, suddenly deciding to use him for herding practice. He drove Blackface at a flat-out gallop across the desert, nipping his rump whenever he faltered, making him jump boulders, scrabble through bushes, scratch himself on cactus spines he hadn't time to avoid, thrusting ahead to cut him off and turn him in this direction and that as the whim took him, squealin a tone that wouldn't have intimidated any mare but which completely stunned Blackface with terror. When he could find voice he screamed out desperately for the grey mare to come to his rescue, and although she was a long way off she heard him and came galloping to see what was happening.

Her sudden movement was the signal for panic in the whole herd. They stampeded after the lead mare and the bay stallion bellowed out his rage as he sought to bring them back. By the time he had reached the instigator of all the trouble the grey mare had already punished him and was nuzzling the trembling, sweating Blackface all over to reassure both him and herself.

All the herd had stopped its flight and the mares stood waiting for the stallion, flanks heaving, ears strained, eyes wide, none of them knowing what had frightened them. The stallion came snorting round them and drove them back to their original grazing place, nipping one, threatening another, and in his rage keeping them on the move for half an hour, until his anger had been worked out of him. By the time he had finished they were all exhausted, not least the foals whose legs and flanks trembled with the effort of running so long beside their dams.

When Blackface woke up after a very long slumber he still had the memory of his fright and he went in search of the pinto to chase it out of himself by trying to intimidate him. But the pinto gave as good as he got and after a few minutes they were pursuing each other as they always did, taking it in turns to catch and be caught in a very amicable fashion.

The bay stallion drove both White Blaze and the buckskin off his territory and the only other colt left in the herd was the pink sorrel who, though now a three-year-old, was no kind of trouble-maker and showed very little stallion instinct. He was the second most inferior member of the herd, the palomino being the only one beneath him, and when Blackface and the pinto began their tussles and scrapes he would sometimes join in after wistfully watching them for a while. At first the two foals were frightened of him, rushing back to their dams when this almost full-grown colt came barging in on them, but they soon learned that he was fun to play with, except that they always tired before he did and therefore never gained the advantage over him.

In spite of their boldness, Blackface and the pinto never instigated any mock battles with the sorrel and they would immediately back down when he tried to involve them in face-to-face encounters. Their subservience to him did a lot for the sorrel colt's ego. For once he wasn't being pushed around by others. However, he was too good-natured to grow mean about it and, once the three of them had learned to understand each other, they indulged in many a chase that set all the mares and fillies on edge, sometimes incurring the wrath of the stallion.

There were painful lessons to be learnt as well as exciting ones. For a week Blackface's muzzle was swollen with cactus spines that drove him mad with irritation. He rubbed and rolled his nose all over the ground until they eventually came out but in the meantime every day was a misery to him. Another time he almost lost the sight of one eye as a result of nibbling inquisitively among the blind prickly pear whose artfully concealed spines he hadn't been aware of until it was too late. His eye swelled and closed up and the left side of his face ran with fly-ridden pus until, almost miraculously, it healed itself. Nature was a far harder taskmaster than any of his own kind.

5

When the bay stallion brought his mares back to the desert, all but the palomino were fat and in good condition. Their mustang bodies had quickly responded to the surfeit of grazing that might have caused colic or lameness in less hardy creatures but served only to prepare them for the deprivations ahead. But the palomino was no mustang, and the birth of Blackface at the end of a rigorous year had robbed her of more strength than she could afford to lose.

After surrendering her own foal to the grey, in her frustration and sense of loss she had taken to the sorrel mare's new filly, encouraging her to nurse whenever she wished. The palomino, the sorrel and her offspring had formed a group within a group. They always grazed together, slept close, groomed each other and, in the long, hot afternoons stood in a circle, heads together, keeping the flies off each other's rumps with their tails. They went to water together, the sorrel mare in the lead, the foal beside her and her bay yearling just behind, then the palomino, with the sorrel colt bringing up the rear, instinctively taking the stallion position although he still had no real ambition to steal the four females for himself.

The palomino had no memory now of Blackface and was as afraid of him as she was of the mare who had stolen him. Her eyes watched and her ears listened only for the sorrel's filly foal, and the two mares took it in turn to clean and nurse her. There was no jealousy between them; the palomino never attempted to steal the foal for herself and made no pretence to any but the most inferior position in their little group. The foal, a pink-nosed bay, did well with this arrangement, even though the palomino had little milk to offer, and it brought no hardship to the sorrel. But the palomino grazed all summer just to feed little Pink Nose.

She was still in milk when it was time to return to the mountains, and bones stared through the hide whose gold colouring was as faded as her beauty. She felt so weak that she was afraid of lying down at night and dozed rather than slept, spending most nights acting as watchdog because this was always the duty of the last one standing. Cold winds, cold days, even colder nights, and the necessity of searching long for every mouthful of fodder took their toll on her, but still she offered herself whenever Pink Nose came nuzzling up for an extra mouthful.

The trek across cracked and stony ground – completely waterless, the wind blowing against them, the cold's grip growing stronger and stronger and the grazing almost non-existent – was hard enough for horses in good condition. For the palomino it entailed supreme effort, calling on resources never replaced. She struggled to keep in line behind the sorrel's yearling and in front of the colt, but the pace was too keen for her. She got further and further behind, and although the stallion harried her over several miles, he eventually left her to herself. He had no particular affection for her and a weak mare was a danger to all the rest. The herd was only as strong as its individual members.

Now and again he halted to look back at her as she dragged along with lowered head and mechanically moving legs, his ears pricking and flattening with annoyance and indecision. To give up on a mare was against his nature but his instinct to shun all weakness was equally strong.

She managed to catch up with them before dawn because they had stopped to graze and rest and she hadn't. She came among them at a racking trot, nostrils wide and strained in this last effort of hers, eyes bulging with fear – the fear of not being able to make it, of being left behind. Pink Nose gambolled forward, eager to guzzle as always, but the palomino had hardly brushed her nose against her when the sorrel mare lunged at her with bared incisors, making her jump away. Like the stallion, she could sense and was afraid of the palomino's weakness. When they all moved off again the golden mare made no attempt to follow. She knew when she was beaten.

Much later that day she turned back towards the desert water-hole where so often she had stood to quench her thirst and gratefully enjoy the pleasure it gave her. She met up with White Blaze and the buckskin who were trailing the herd. They took charge of her for a few days, fighting each other for possession of her, but when they too sensed her weakness they abruptly abandoned her and went after the herd again.

It didn't snow in the desert but the ground was frozen and at night the moon gleamed on frost-coated rocks. Alone, the palomino hardly even dozed, listening with frightened quiverings to the yap of the coyote, the sharp scream of a hunted rabbit, the caterwaul of a bobcat. She looked silver in the moonlight, cold as the frost, still as the stone. During one of these silvery, stone-cold nights a pack of coyotes surrounded her. She voiced one long, desperate whinny before doubling up for them.

She was still wearing Don Rafael's leather head-collar. Its stitching mostly rotted away, it was ready to fall apart, as unfitted as she was for survival without human care in so harsh a place.

PART THREE
Survival

I

Blackface was already weaned by the time his foster mother produced another foal, and his spirit of independence was such that he hardly missed her while she was away from the herd. The excitement of rediscovering the desert, which he could hardly recall from his early months, entirely engrossed him. He and the pinto rushed about, eyes bright, ears never still, nostrils wide, examining every rock, tree, bush and wild flower. The pinto's mother also foaled again so the two youngsters, finding themselves alone and even unwanted when at last their respective dams returned, spent more and more time together, hardly able to stop racing about over the endless desert expanse after so long a confinement at the foot of the *barranca*. Food was less important to them than their games, so they grazed in snatches and devoted the long summer afternoons to heavy slumber, bellies facing the sun, necks and limbs stretched out in foal-like abandon.

The palomino's colt was a scarecrow-looking creature at the start of his second year, with every rib well marked through his oatmeal yellow coat, his head seeming too big for his almost fleshless frame. Gone was the plumpness of his milk days and, even though the long valley winter rounded out the mares and fillies again, the young colt burned up all his energy in madcap games and hardly put on an ounce of flesh. However, his bones grew, his muscles developed and his skin glowed with well-being in spite of his skeletal appearance. His mane and tail were jet black, as was his muzzle, and then the black of his nose and cheekbones was interspersed with oatmeal-coloured hairs in such a way that from glossy black his face gradually lightened to almost pure oatmeal again, just above the eyes whose lashes were long and black. His ears were oatmeal, bordered with black as if outlined by an artist's brush, and his neck and breast were mottled in varying shades of light and dark, as were his hind-quarters. In the dappled shadows of oak trees and *manzanita* he could have been taken for a grey, but in the desert his colouring was almost that of the very earth.

His spirit was as brash and uncontrolled as his movements, still almost as clumsy as a foal's, and when that summer started he had respect for only two members of the herd — the grey mare and his sire. For the former his respect was tinged with such familiarity that her occasional nips and warnings were forgotten almost as soon as they were registered, whereas the stallion was so remote a being that Blackface's behaviour towards him was conditioned by herd reflex. He had learned in just one year the meaning of every ear movement, the exact message in every snort, squeal, grunt or shake of the stallion's head, and he had learned just as quickly how to react. But although until now he had responded with instinctive submissiveness whenever the stallion happened to cross his path, by the beginning of his second year the bumptious, provocative audacity that his health, high spirits and youth stimulated made him forget all that he had learned.

Because of this it was to be a hard summer for Blackface and his pinto companion, whose spirits were just as high and sense of self-importance equally unassailable. Both had spent the last six months causing havoc among the mares and fillies, fleeing to the protection of their mothers if things got out of hand, but soon saucily dancing forth again for another round of teasings. Until now the grey mare had always defended Blackface and he had seen how every mare gave way to her and therefore to him. When the new foals were brought into the herd he received the first hard knocks of his life.

With his natural curiosity he was among the first to dash forward to inspect them and let them know how important he was. Mares that had previously moved away at his approach now came forward with bared teeth, or lashed out with hind legs when he drew too close in defiance of warning signals in which he didn't really believe. It took several kicks on his breast and shoulders and two deep bites on his rump for him to learn that he was no longer inviolable and, worse still, that not even his dam would race to get him out of scrapes. She had a filly foal of dark mahogany to care for and whenever Blackface drew close to this wobbly, curious-looking creature she warned him off with flattened ears and bared incisors, her wicked expression now turned on him as much as on any other.

He discovered that as a yearling he was considered a nuisance by all the mares and fillies, a nuisance they were no longer obliged to tolerate. His friendly battles with the pinto hadn't taught him how to dodge fast enough from a genuine attack, and his various encounters left him both lame and highly disconcerted. Moreover, as the stallion came among his females to be close to them through this period of birthing and new breeding, Blackface found himself being chased by him from one place to another, and warned away from any mare in season, however innocent might be the cause of his presence. If the mares didn't really frighten him, the stallion did, so malevolent was the promise in his flattened ears and snaking head.

That summer he did a lot of running away, with bruises and bites to remind him when he had forgotten that he was no longer inviolable. If he did so much running away it was because, in spite of the reminders, he was always coming back, sometimes overcome by curiosity, other times from

73

sheer devilment. He acquired some wariness, learning just how close the stallion would allow him while courting a female, and how much a mare would permit in an effort to play with her foal.

The stallion was at his most cantankerous. He had thrust out both his two-year-old colts almost on arrival in the desert and they had met up with Black Legs and the buckskin who continued to follow the herd from a distance. White Blaze had choked to death on prickly pear that winter but there was still a band of four to trespass on the bay stallion's territory and almost every other day they gave him a skirmish, as much out of sheer high spirits as in any hope of stealing his mares. Sometimes all four would attack him at once; occasionally Black Legs, now a powerful-looking four-year-old, would sally forth alone in search of a straying mare, watched from a distance by the others; but however they came at him the bay stallion was more than a match for them.

The black stallion also watched the herd's movements from a distance. He had lost the two fillies of the previous summer but, though alone, he had no wish to join Black Legs's band. He hung around hopefully and a couple of times put the younger studs to flight, then disappeared as elusively as he had come after offering only a token display of animosity towards the bay stallion.

Against all these would-be thieves the stallion that year had an ally in the sorrel colt who was now a four-year-old and still within the herd because of his submissive, unaggressive nature. Very unobtrusively he had appropriated two females, both daughters of the bay stallion and one his own sister, grazing always alongside them, making grooming partners of them, gradually asserting his authority over them. His dam and other sister, Pink Nose, had been part of this little family all winter through, but both had been reclaimed by the stallion at the start of the breeding season. No battle had taken place. Just as soon as the stallion came up at a collected trot, head high, neck flexed, showing how prepared he was to crush any opposition, the sorrel colt moved away, followed by the two fillies. His dam stood her ground, owing allegiance to the bay stallion, and young Pink Nose, still not completely weaned, stayed with her. The stallion sniffed them all over, snorting, grunting, stamping a forefoot impatiently until satisfying himself that he had what belonged to him, and the sorrel colt watched from a distance with a filly on either flank just behind him.

This time when the stallion came to inspect them the sorrel stood his ground, willing for the first time in his four years to defend a reasonable demand. The bay made a show of authority to remind him who was boss but then turned to drive the mare back to the herd, having learnt from hard experience that his young daughters were more trouble than they were worth.

The two families continued to share the same watering place and even the same grazing, and when Black Legs came along with challenging scream and defiantly tossing head, backed up by the other outcasts, both the bay and the sorrel chased them off.

The sorrel was very possessive of his first females and tolerated Blackface's proximity no better than the bay stallion did. The days when he had attacked the two youngsters in play were over and now there was nothing to be done with him but keep out of his way. But Blackface was too high spirited to be disconsolate for long and when he was tired of being threatened or chased he always had the pinto on whom to take out his high spirits.

The two battled together all summer long, trying to force each other to the ground with neck movements, biting each other's muzzles, attacking forelegs, shoulder or ribs, learning to snap like lightning and yet avoid each other's bites. There was never any real victor, though sometimes one might reel away from an exuberant kick he hadn't managed to avoid, and after a while they would be grazing side by side or nibbling each other's rumps.

When winter came foalhood was a long way behind them both.

2

By the start of his third summer Blackface was a real trouble-maker. The winter in the canyon was far too long for him. There was no room to stretch his legs into a gallop and yet the plentiful grazing so filled him with energy that all he wanted to do was race about and look for mischief. When at last he was back in the desert again nothing could contain his ardent joy at being alive. Dynamic, almost electric power filled his being, compelling him to ever increasing restlessness, and his games with the pinto were no longer enough. He wanted a whole herd to command.

As a two-year-old he was still all ribs, long legs and heavy mane, but now there was a grace and determination in his movements that all the previous months of learning, growing and playing had gradually given him. His long, fine neck was thickening with muscles built up by the constant flexing of his big, proud head, which he tossed and snaked and imperiously tucked in during mock battles with the pinto. His hard black legs, grey-scarred by cactus spines, were well muscled from so much rearing, striking and impatient pawing, and even his voice was different. The high-sounding neighs and squeals of his early youth had dropped in tone and now he could produce sounds from deep inside him, stallion snorts and grunts for showing off, and a ringing, challenging roar which would make the whole herd look up to stare at him in startled expectation.

One day he took it into his head that the water-hole was his property alone and that no other horse should approach it. He stayed very close to it all day, now and again circling the bit of territory he had claimed to mark it as his own, head held high, ears alert, as he constantly watched the scattered, grazing herd. The bay stallion that day was more interested in a buckskin mare near foaling than in one of his upstart youngsters, so there was none to challenge his command.

The pinto came up to entice him into a game but, after hanging around for a while, he wandered off again, sensing Blackface's aggressive mood and not particularly keen to question it. Blackface watched him belligerently the whole time.

Later one of the mares approached, accompanied by her yearling daughter. This dun was a compliant creature, never one to question the authority of flattened ears and mean expression. She was thirsty, she needed a drink, but she wasn't prepared to risk a bite for it. Blackface's arrogant prancing round the water-hole soon sent her away. Later in the afternoon a strange buckskin colt came to drink there and with an impressive show of strength Blackface drove him off, biting his rump and chasing after him for half a mile even though the stranger made no effort to defend himself. He was too young yet to know when to accept another's defeat, and only abandoned the pursuit when the territory he had claimed seemed dangerously far away.

This little incident added to Blackface's confidence so that by the time the mares started to return to the water-hole for their customary evening drink he was ready with a great show of bravado to keep them away. The high, showy trot he had developed for just such an occasion as this, and his threatening stallion snorts, certainly brought them to a halt. Mares and youngsters all stopped to stare uncertainly at him. Blackface sensed their indecision and he knew he had won. None dared approach. The water-hole was his.

Suddenly the grey lead mare appeared. He had forgotten about her, forgotten too that if the mares hadn't come to drink it was because they were waiting for her to go first rather than because they were frightened of him. Flattening her ears, she thrust straight past him and with her came the mahogany filly, now a graceful yearling but as mean as her mother. This was Blackface's first real test. Did he dare risk a confrontation with these two?

He decided that discretion was the better part of valour in their case but, to make up for this, he flung himself at White Patch to keep her from following. She wheeled away from his teeth but quickly turned to lash out with her hind legs, which he only just managed to avoid, and then she too, together with her own filly, was at the water-hole beside the grey.

Angry now, somewhat unnerved by their unceremonious scorn of him, Blackface descended on the lesser mares, determined to gain some sort of recognition for his claim, and a wild skirmish developed as some resented it and others fled.

A sense of power surged through him as he recklessly chased colts and fillies and two of the mares off his territory, squealing and snorting, but whenever he glanced back at the water-hole he knew his victory wasn't complete. Sheer numbers alone were defeating him. Flushed with his minor victories, he decided to try new tactics, dropping his head snake-like as he bore down on the bunch of animals at the water, sure that this would make them budge. But hardly had he dropped his head before the bay stallion was upon him, threatening him with a brassy neigh, knocking him sideways as their shoulders clashed. Blackface hit the ground very hard and before he could get up the stallion was tearing at his mane with furious teeth, his hooves ready to crash into him at the slightest opposition. Ignominiously he scrabbled up and away, and from a distance watched the mares and youngsters settle themselves round the water-hole, his water-hole, to drink.

From claiming territory Blackface very soon progressed to trying to claim mares. At first, in his blatant conceit, his plan was to take the whole herd. In defiance of the stallion he would gallop round the mares in a wide arc, neighing orders to them, giddy with the sense of power that surged through him as he saw how they began running together from different directions, instinctively obedient to his commands. But his glorious moments were never more than that. In no time at all the bay stallion would be in pursuit of him, ready to pound or bite him into submission. Then for a few days Blackface would behave himself, stiff perhaps with bruises, until once again the urge to try out his strength became too much for him.

Next he picked on the sorrel stallion's family, sensing that this animal had not his sire's blasting temperament. He galloped round and round the whole bunch – there were three fillies now, one of them with a colt foal – and from time to time the flustered sorrel made rushes at him, refusing to give ground but unable to frighten him away. Blackface was convinced he had captured the entire family. The fillies watched him with intense curiosity, mesmerized perhaps by his constant circling. Their ears quivered in expectation as he suddenly halted and began to show off, rearing, squealing, challenging the sorrel to do his worst. The sorrel was no great battler. He had won his few fillies by bluff alone and it was with bluff that he outwitted Blackface now, stepping forward a few paces to press his head against the other's while sending his fillies off at a gallop with his warning snorts. Before Blackface could react the sorrel had turned and was galloping after them and the next the colt knew was that he was alone, his captured band already a quarter of a mile away, no longer his.

Through all these frustrations Blackface learned a lot,

except that he didn't know he was learning and needed to repeat his same actions time and again before drawing any conclusions from them. Thus he was always claiming new patches and being chased from them, capturing mares and as quickly losing them, throwing all his strength and ardour into every action and being outwitted or outfaced at every turn.

If he had believed that the mares and fillies would clamour for his attention, he was quickly disillusioned for, much as he would pursue them whenever the bay stallion was out of reach, they were as likely to turn on him with waspish temper as with any friendliness and their hooves and teeth were even more relentless than the stallion's.

This last was the most difficult for him to understand for he was intensely attracted to the mares at all times, except when engaged in defending a patch of his own ground. His urge to possess them was constant and with this end in view he would invite their attentions, displaying himself before them with arched neck and high-stepping trot, trying to get close enough to nibble their skin and sniff them all over, carelessly abandoning all thoughts of self-defence. He usually got kicked for his efforts if he didn't manage to jump out of the way in time but, with his youthful impetuosity and self-assurance, he would be back a moment later to try again, until eventually either a mare really hurt him or the stallion got wise to his actions and came galloping up to drive him away.

The younger fillies were more likely to receive him with some excitement, and now and again he almost got away with herding off one or another. Sometimes he and the pinto tried their tricks together, but sooner or later the stallion always discovered them and put an end to their triumph.

Though not entirely banished from the herd, both colts were very much outsiders now, from choice as much as necessity. There was no fun in being among the staid, fat-bellied, ill-humoured mares whose only interests were to graze and care for their offspring. When not engaged in any particular mischief, Blackface preferred to flank the grazing herd at a suitable distance from his sire. Like this he could believe himself to be equally responsible for the mares and was constantly watching for the opportunity to make off with one of the stragglers. While he kept at a distance the bay stallion took little notice of him. He had the pinto to worry about, as well as the yearling colts who sometimes got out of hand, and although he and the sorrel stallion had an amicable arrangement, his keen gaze was as much on him as anywhere else. He also had to keep all the surrounding countryside under constant surveillance because a lone stallion, or even a whole bunch of young studs, could suddenly appear to challenge him. Having to snatch his food in mouthfuls, he didn't waste energy unnecessarily, and so long as Blackface kept out of his way and caused no trouble he left him alone.

The buckskin mare foaled a dark bay colt and on the third day brought him back to the herd. Blackface happened to see her first, when she was still a good two miles from the other mares, and quickly he moved to meet her. His show of bravado as he approached stopped her in her tracks and she watched him with great caution, fearful for her foal.

Blackface had no interest in the foal, caring only about the mare. He had her completely to himself and was all eagerness to overcome any opposition. He disregarded the sharp, threatening squeals she uttered to hold him at bay and boldly ignored her flattened ears, taking her nervousness to be easily overcome indecision. He grabbed her withers in an intended caress, grunting forceful stallion commands, completely carried away by the excitement of the moment. She retaliated with bared teeth but he cared very little about her protests, his body hardened against kicks and bites, and he towered over her, angrily biting her neck to subdue her, too intent upon his purpose to accept any rejection. The foal clung to her with wide-eyed fear, getting under Blackface's legs, unwittingly aggravating him. Several times the colt nosed him impatiently out of the way, knocking him over with his brusque haste, and every time the mare made a sharp dash to escape, Blackface shouldered her furiously to a standstill, determined to have his way.

By now the bay stallion had become aware of the buckskin's predicament and he rocketed to her rescue, roaring the most thunderous threats as he swirled round them to a halt. Blackface's blood was up. The mare was almost his and in his hot-headed excitement he wasn't going to give her up. What cared he for the bay stallion just then? He wanted his own way.

There was a circling, whirling, screaming as the two male animals confronted each other without any preliminary show and their dark bodies almost disappeared in the cloud of dust kicked up by their raging hooves. This close *mêlée* only lasted half a minute, Blackface being completely routed by the teeth that slashed open his jaw and tore out a great hunk of mane almost before he could realize the battle had started. He hung on for a moment, unable to back away, and then he fled with a terror as great as that of his foalhood when the buckskin had chased him, the stallion pounding along beside him, still ripping out chunks of hair and skin.

Blackface ran the race of his life, but for all his youth and his longer legs he couldn't outrun the frenziedly incensed bay who every now and then slashed at him again. It seemed as if his lungs would burst and still he would fall beneath the other's hooves, except that of a sudden the bay tired of the chase and gave it up, turning to gallop back to the lone mare and her foal. Blackface ran on a bit further and when at last he stopped, he could hardly hold up his head, such was his exhaustion. His whole body was soaked with sweat, his breath came in shuddering gasps through open jaws and widely strained nostrils, his legs trembled and he could hardly see. As yet he was unaware of all his wounds, although his jaw was already stiffening. For the next few hours he didn't move, head hanging low, all his pride gone.

3

That was the end of Blackface's life as a member of the bay stallion's family, and the beginning of a long period of bachelorhood. The first days were very hard for him because in all his life he had never been alone, in strange territory, with no instinctive sense of protection in numbers. As an accepted member of the bay stallion's band it was easy for him to be self-confident, his independence bolstered by an unchanging rhythm he had never questioned, anchored to habits and routine set by others who had gone before him. Now he was free from his sire's dominance – the whole desert stretched away before him – and every instinct urged him to return.

He was suddenly aware that behind each rock and cactus plant there might be a cougar or a rattlesnake; that in the unseen dips any and every unknowable danger could be lurking; and his ears worked, his nostrils flared, his eyes unceasingly watched between every single mouthful of food. The slightest unexpected sound or movement – the screech of a bird, the sudden fall of a decayed branch – jerked him into flight and he would stare about with heaving flanks and nervous hooves, anticipating everything, not knowing why he was frightened.

It rained every day so the grazing was good, grass and flowers sprouting everywhere, and when he was thirsty he drank from the shallow lakes before they vanished. He rolled in the mud to keep the flies off his wounds but there was no joy in his rolling. Down on the ground, legs in the air, his neck and belly were dangerously exposed. Among the herd, in his youthful abandon, this had never worried him before. There was always some animal on the lookout. It was a thing instinctively accepted, instinctively known. On his own he needed the sight of a dozen pairs of eyes, the alertness of as many ears, a never ceasing vigilance. He gave up lying down to sleep, dozing in snatches on his feet, and he tired of trying to groom his own back.

Worst of all there were no mares or fillies to capture, to dominate, to run rings round. At the beginning of each day he would raise his head and let out long, throaty whinnies to tell the lonely desert that everything there was his, but by nightfall he would be just a little closer to his sire's grazing grounds. By the time the herd was within his reach he gave up his stallion cries, contenting himself with surveying the distant mares and youngsters with eager eyes and a longing deep within him which burst out in soft, throaty whickers.

The stallion saw him and threw up his head to give full throat to a loud brassy neigh of warning and Blackface, his jaw still swollen and painful, conscious of the stiff sores from half a dozen bites along his back, dropped his head and moved off. He circled round the herd at a great distance, but the bay stallion knew of his presence and now and then sent a battle cry in his direction.

Back on his old territory Blackface lost his fears. Here the agaves sheltered no secret danger; here there were no coyotes panting in the shade of the prickly pear; and, when at last one morning just before dawn he ventured to drink at the water-hole and there was none to challenge his action, his self-confidence returned. He stood there for a long time, ears alert but no longer anxious, letting the water slide through his teeth very much in the manner of the palomino, savouring his first long, relaxed watering in many days. Before the grey lead mare took the others to the same place

86

he had gone, but the bay stallion knew he had been there. He meticulously sniffed all the ground, knowing exactly where Blackface had stood and trod, and when he found the piles of dung the colt had defiantly left he carefully covered them with his own.

Being back within the vicinity of the herd, though no longer a member of it, brought a renewal of spirit to the black and yellow colt. Once again he grazed and galloped with abandon, but although he often watched the mares with overwhelming interest, he made no attempt to steal them or even call them. One thing at least he had learnt was that the bay stallion was far too great an opponent to reckon with just yet. But he called to the pinto and the stallion recognized the different sound in his voice and ignored him. The pinto galloped to meet him and the two plunged into a wild game of rearing and kicking just as soon as they had exchanged greetings. They cantered for several miles, side by side, wrestling with each other's heads without altering their pace, and when the pinto was tired of it all he went back to the herd.

Day after day they raced and fought with each other and when the sun was hot they stood nose to tail as they had always done, swishing off each other's flies, nibbling each other's rough patches. Sometimes they were angry with each other, exchanging baleful glances with flattened ears and swishing tails. Blackface, believing he had kidnapped the pinto from the herd, wanted to enforce his superiority by driving his companion wherever the fancy took him, but the pinto hadn't accepted this view of things at all and wouldn't be herded anywhere. So they swung their heads menacingly at each other and stubbornly each stood his ground until both forgot and they were friends again.

The pinto stopped returning to the herd when he was tired. The two of them trekked to the water-hole each day just before dawn and then they would be miles away, waking up the birds, startling scorpions, lizards, spiders with the thunder of their hooves over the hard ground. Once they were attacked by Black Legs who had given up his association with his outlawed half-brothers and now roamed alone, strong and mean and hungry for mares. He chased them both with murderous intent, fearing their possible intervention in his plans, and neither tried to outface him. They watched him challenge the bay stallion only a few days later.

The battle was short, the bay using different tactics for this formidable-looking son of his. He was now entering his fifteenth year, and although he was still strong and swift he was growing cautious and had no illusions about the necessity of gaining a quick advantage. Instead of rushing forward to meet Black Legs he herded up his mares and youngsters and drove them off under the grey mare's leadership. Then, well within his own safe territory, he returned Black Legs's ringing challenge, defying him to come close.

No animal feels entirely safe in another's territory and the further he strays into it the more he is psychologically unprepared for battle. He finds it more necessary to defend himself than attack and is very much aware that he's a long way from safety. The bay stallion had learned all the tricks in his many years, and by the time he gave up following his herd and turned to face his challenger, Black Legs had already half lost the contest. Still he put up a brave show and one of his blows left the bay stallion lame for a week. So total was his acceptance of defeat, however, that he didn't return to press his advantage in these circumstances. Instead, he attacked the sorrel stallion and took his three fillies and foal from him. On his own the sorrel stood little chance against a determined opponent, and this time the bay hadn't felt disposed to help him.

The sorrel was completely lost without his family. He wasn't a spirited fighter and knew only too well his limitations. For some time he followed after Black Legs, as did

Blackface and the pinto whose curiosity was greater than any sense of danger just then, but none of them dared grow very close. The sorrel joined up with the two colts but their games and races were too high-spirited for him and eventually, resigned to his loss, he went back to the bay stallion's herd, hanging uncertainly about its fringes and only gradually reincorporating himself in its structure. Perhaps he had hopes of getting himself another group of fillies as he had done before. Whatever his intentions the bay stallion still didn't consider him a threat although he chased him around for a few days, biting his mane and withers until satisfied of the sorrel's complete submission.

Black Legs had trouble with his fillies at first. They wanted to return to their old grazing grounds and were constantly trying to break away. Blackface and the pinto called often to them, tossing their heads and putting on a display of strength as close as they dared before dashing off at the first threat from Black Legs. He was extremely nervous of losing his captives and hardly let them break out of a tight bunch all day long, adding to their irritation. However, as the days passed and the only challengers around were the two colts, he gradually relaxed and let them relax too.

4

In this manner the summer passed, the two colts completely carefree and independent of the herd as long as they had each other. They roamed widely and got themselves chased by one stallion or another, but eventually they always came back to their home territory because it was still the core of their existence. When the herd moved off towards its wintering ground, Blackface and the pinto followed at half a day's distance.

They had watered at dawn as usual and then discovered that the bay stallion and his band had gone. They travelled much faster than the mares and foals, both of them anxious not to be left behind, and eventually caught up with them at the next watering place which was the stream at the canyon's ragged edge. In their eagerness they had forgotten that they no longer belonged to the herd and they whinnied loud greetings to the relaxed mares and youngsters, overjoyed to see them all again. Just now they weren't young stallions, proud and challenging, but two erring brothers relieved to be back with the family.

The mares welcomed them quite cordially, responding to their innocent greetings with a chorus of whinnies, and there was a good bit of blowing and squealing as more personal greetings were exchanged. The sorrel stallion stood apart, ears flattened, giving warning grunts and shaking his head, but they cared little for his disapproval. The bay stallion was a different matter. While the mares drank and grazed near the stream, he had gone ahead to examine the terrain. The noisy greetings soon brought him back and when he saw the two youngsters touching noses with the mares, rubbing heads against necks, acting as if they had never been away from the family, he plunged wrathfully among them all, shouldering aside mares and colts to reach the two outcasts more quickly.

Too surprised to be able to dash for safety, their immediate reaction was to plead submissiveness, dropping their heads and ears, flattening their tails. This indeed placated the stallion somewhat, preventing him from attacking them with his usual ferocity, but still he would not have them in the herd. Ignoring them for a moment, he turned back to the mares, dropping his head low in the signal for them all to start moving, and as quickly as possible if they didn't want to be bitten.

In a hasty, nervous bunch, tight behind the grey lead mare, they flustered into the stream which dropped steeply away into the canyon, and the stallion brought up the rear, head lifted now as he whinnied out loud threats to them all. Blackface and the pinto drew close together, both too frightened to comfort each other except in this small way. The stallion clambered back over the rim, chest and legs dark with splashings, and there he stood, threatening and formidable, as hard and craggy in silhouette as the very walls of the *barranca*. For a long while he gazed at his sons, aware all the time of the progress of the mares down into the gorge, the colts aware too that the herd was getting farther and farther away and that they couldn't join it. They didn't return the bay stallion's gaze, both of them intent on making themselves look as insignificant and innocent as possible. Then suddenly the stallion left them, plunging after his mares, but such was his power that until some time after he had gone the two colts did not move.

They drank from the stream, then they went to look over

the canyon's edge. The mares were no longer in sight, hidden in shadows or by overhanging rocks, but they knew which way they had gone because they themselves had twice been part of that long descent. Blackface began grazing but the pinto's attention was still with the herd after which he whickered with longing in both voice and pricked ears.

It was cold at the top of the *barranca*. The wind blew fiercely, touched with ice, and there was nowhere to escape it except within the deep mouth of the silent gorge. The pinto was the first to make up his mind, habit stronger than the memory of the recent confrontation with the stallion, and Blackface followed him. Their confidence grew as they descended unchallenged to the bottom of the gorge and reached the swift but shallow river, and they plunged into its green waters with carefree eagerness, remembering only the way ahead and the lush valley awaiting them.

The dark came rapidly. High above them was the moon but in the narrow, twisting gorge, overhung with rocks and tree roots, blackness and shadows and the sound of running water was all about them. Bats jerked close about their heads but they plunged on because there was no stopping place. Weary but hopeful, tails heavy and dripping, they reached the valley at last. Here moonlight reflected on the water, on the light and dark coloured mares and colts, giving outlines to trees and reeds, mellowing the rocky walls. Again they whinnied out their greetings, no thought of caution in their gladness to be safe, but before they were halfway towards the herd the bay stallion was cutting across the space between them, head low and angry looking.

They made all the right submissive gestures, the pinto going so far as to twist up his tongue in sucking sounds, so desperate was he to be accepted again, but there was no relenting. This time he wasn't protecting his mares so much as his territory. The valley was small, too small to be shared with troublesome firebrands whose closeness he could only tolerate at the right critical distance. Instinct to protect these two sons of his had vanished just as soon as they could lift their heads as high as he did and make stallion calls almost as ringing as his own. Whenever they were near there was disunity and therefore danger for his herd, and so he chased them mercilessly from his valley in spite of their willingness to submit.

Blackface momentarily withstood him, more from fear than bravado, kicking out backwards before dashing after the pinto. They shouldered each other through the crevice, not stopping till they were on the steep rockface again, alone in the noisy darkness, and there they spent the rest of the night, vainly searching for grazing, slipping and sliding and exerting all their muscles on this terrain only fit for goats and cougars.

The next day they followed the river downstream, looking for another valley like the one that was lost to them, but not finding even the barest grazing. In places the river was blocked by rockslides, forcing them to turn back and look for other ways of passing. They nibbled for a time at a mound of broken *carrizo*, but the splintery, cane-like quality of the drying reeds, which had been washed up over the rocks by high flood waters, was too unpalatable, hungry as they were. And this was all they found as they splashed their way up and down the river, floundering over slippery boulders, kicking wildly as they suddenly plunged out of their depth, pausing to regain strength whenever they found a patch of beach clinging to the foot of the rocks.

In the end they had no alternative but to abandon the *barranca*, which was only safe and warm in the bay stallion's valley. Their gait was weary and subdued as they took the trail back to the top, digging in the points of their hooves to stop themselves slipping, and many times they halted to look back, still drawn to their old companions.

They looked for other ways down into the *barranca* and

spent many days following the trails of sheep and mule-deer. On two separate occasions they were attacked by cougars when only their alertness and speed saved them. The night temperatures were well below freezing and often they hardly felt the sun because of the thick fogs now rolling across the mountains, heralding the long deep winter. Icicles hung from their ears, under their chins, in their manes and tails. Then it began to snow and the snow came with the same fury as the rainstorms of the desert, driving, blinding, changing the landscape they knew into a world of dazzling strangeness where they stumbled over unseen rocks, bruising their heels, and searched hopelessly for grazing.

The snow drove them off the mountain at last, back to the desert where at least there were no trees among whose branches cougars could hide to spring out on them and where they could race without stumbling. What if the cold of the night almost stilled the blood in their veins? As soon as the sun was up Blackface was rearing over the slowly stretching pinto, defying him to question his authority, or the pinto was tossing his head and stamping a challenging hoof, because their battles for supremacy never ended. There were short truces for grazing and watering, for dozing and grooming, and even for sullen lack of interest in each other when perhaps bodies were bruised or spirits were sore, but neither cold nor hunger could diminish them for long.

Their bodies grew leaner and harder, their muscles more supple, their senses more alert, nature stripping away everything not required for their survival, including any gentleness of temper. There were no rounded contours, smooth angles, polished skins to soften the effects of their stark existence, but still there was a kind of defiant beauty in their scarred gauntness, in the carriage of their big, proud heads and wild expressions.

95

5

That winter Blackface and the pinto roamed further from their home territory than they had ever done in any of their wanderings, driven by hunger rather than any urge to find new places. With the end of the rainy season the desert had soon lost its flowers and its greenness, and very soon all the land within grazing distance of the water-hole was completely bare as far as the horses were concerned. They were reduced to foraging on the fallen pads of blind prickly pear, suffering the pain and irritation of the thousand tiny brown barbs that worked themselves into the softer parts of their mouths, and still they were hungry. They wandered into Black Legs's territory, only to find it as bare as the bay stallion's, and when he chased them away they didn't go back because there was nothing to steal. Their wanderings were no more than a search for food, their direction controlled by the wind which they kept to their backs as much as possible.

They met up with the buckskin who was now a wiry little four-year-old and the leader of his three-colt band. The buckskin had the advantage because he saw them first but he approached them in a friendly manner, his rapid ear movements indicating at the same time that his friendliness depended on their accepting his superiority. Both Blackface and the pinto were inexperienced enough to be intimidated by this approach. They nervously allowed him to sniff them all over, the other colts watching from a distance, but Blackface laid back his ears, ready to defend himself should the buckskin's manner change. His tail swished and he drew back his lips as his confidence returned and this defiant show made the buckskin lunge with bared teeth at his haunch. Blackface jumped away to avoid the bite and then the buckskin rounded on the pair of them as if they were recalcitrant mares, head low, ears flat, driving them towards his waiting companions.

These two, a bay and a chestnut, both with long white blazes and white socks – yearling half-brothers that the buckskin had been in charge of since early summer – made little protest at the incorporation of the two newcomers. Both Blackface and the pinto soon asserted their authority over them with very little kicking and biting. Then the five of them settled down to the more serious business of finding something to eat, and only when their bellies were reasonably comfortable did they return to bullying each other.

The two yearlings always came off worst in any skirmishes, with the three other colts often attacking them all at once when their own individual battles were over. Blackface and the pinto went on vying with each other and they took it in turns to challenge the buckskin's rule over them. Whoever was defeated then attacked one of the yearlings and the other three would join in, pulling out chunks of mane but rarely inflicting any damage. Although both yearlings came under attack from the three superior animals, each took advantage of the other's vulnerability, joining in the mobbing whole-heartedly though it might be his turn next.

Such treatment of the two youngest members of the band reduced them to timorous, spiritless creatures and most of the battles between Blackface, the pinto and the buckskin were over the possession of them. One day Blackface would be herding them here and there, giving them no peace, then the buckskin would challenge his right to them and steal them back. Then it would be the pinto's turn to take charge of them and defend them from the other two. They fought for them as if they were fillies instead of colts and the two youngsters behaved with the passivity of females, never attempting to defend themselves and accepting the dominion of all three.

All the time they were travelling further and further from their home territory in search of grazing. They also had to search for water, which was even more difficult to come across. The buckskin showed them how to dig for water, covering long distances with his nose to the ground, then suddenly deciding on a spot for his excavations. He would paw energetically with his hard hoof, when one leg tired using the other, now and again stopping to sniff with alert ears. Sometimes he would dig for hours, watched by the others, until water began to seep through the pulverized earth in sufficient quantity to be sucked up. Blackface and the pinto would threaten each other to be second in the queue. The yearlings came last and equally flattened their ears and tossed their heads at each other until one gave way.

Blackface tired of waiting for the buckskin to find water for them and started digging holes of his own. Sometimes he found water only a little way under the surface but there was one hard, long night when he dug from sunset to sunrise and the hole was a crater big enough to hide half his body before water came. When he found water of his own he wouldn't share it with the pinto until the two yearlings had drunk. After satisfying his own thirst he would deliberately go in search of the youngsters and bring them to his hole, keeping the pinto away with noisy threats.

The buckskin led them far from the land they knew, taking them across stony plains, dangerous with thick patches of low cactus glistening with long, hard needles through which they had to pick their way very carefully. He seemed to know where he was going and kept them on course in spite of the diversions the cactus-covered ground necessitated. There was plenty of mesquite for them to graze on and as they travelled they were aware of a certain humidity in the air even though there was no sight of water. When they dug for it, it came easily.

They left the harmful lechugilla and grusonia cacti behind, coming to an area of white sand dunes, their hooves breaking the neat, wind-rippled patterns. There was plenty of mesquite, yucca and saltbush, but although they managed to fill their bellies and satisfy their thirst, the buckskin was exceedingly nervous and his tense alertness was communicated to the others. Such was their wariness that they spooked at their own shadows. Not knowing what to be frightened of, they found everything frightening, and they even stopped fighting with each other while watching so assiduously for unseen, unknown enemies.

As the sun came up one morning the attention of them all was drawn by a distant shimmering, glassy ribbon. The sky was still very pale and separated from this glassy light by the long, blue-grey mountain range beyond it. All ears were pricked, while wide nostrils breathed in deeply.

The buckskin was the first to start moving towards this ribbon of light. There was confidence in his actions so the others soon followed, strung out in line and moving quickly. The dry, powdery earth gave way to damp ground and soon they were splashing through shallow puddles which heralded the marshy outlets of a lake. Here they drank before tearing greedily at the sedges and grasses growing in thick profusion on every side. Soon they were hock deep in grass which, though dry and yellow, was the best they had tasted in many a month.

This grassy land stretched as far as the horses could see and for days they effortlessly filled their bellies. The buckskin was nervous again, snatching a mouthful of grass, then warily watching in every direction while he chewed and swallowed before reaching for the next. The others took little notice of

99

him this time. All Blackface cared about was displaying himself before his old friend and enemy, taunting him into battle, and the pinto retaliated with equal enthusiasm. They very quickly recovered from the lean times and the winter sun shone on flanks already beginning to fill out. The two yearlings grazed fairly close together and when not grazing they watched the battles between the three older colts and meekly submitted to their herding instincts, having discovered that by so doing they saved themselves from many a mane pulling.

Being the least active of the band they were easy targets for the men on whose cattle lands they were trespassing. They saw the two riders approaching from quite a distance and, having no experience of man, watched in curiosity, ears pricked. The buckskin noticed their stance and followed their line of interest. Even as his warning neigh shrilled out two shots exploded in the air almost simultaneously. The bay yearling went down, struck through the ribs, but the chestnut galloped away, blood pulsing from a wound in his neck.

Now all but the bay were in full flight, making instinctively for the desert land beyond the marshes, led by the buckskin who had lived this experience before. Shots followed them but missed their mark, then there was only the sound of splashing, galloping hooves, strained lungs gasping for air and a screech of quail frightened into the air by the trembling ground.

They fled for several miles until the land with its plentiful water, good grazing and sudden, exploding death was far behind them. The gypsum dunes softened the thud of their hooves which slowed to a canter, then a walk, and then stopped. Snorting and blowing, they drew close to each other for comfort, their hides dark with sweat, the chestnut's shoulder and off foreleg stained with red which left its mark in the white sand. They nickered fearfully at this smell of blood on

one of their number and soon they were hurrying off again, wanting to leave it behind.

Until nightfall they hardly paused but by then they were back in the stony, cactus-covered ground which was so difficult to cross. All were thirsty but none had the energy to dig for water although Blackface made a few token pawings at the ground, watched by the others. The chestnut had been left behind, unable to keep up with their hurried flight, but he found them again in the moonlight and whinnied to them with the longing of a foal needing its dam. His head was very low now and in the moonlight his tatty, much-pulled mane looked like a withered yucca, its spikes collapsed and grey. When the others saw and smelled him they moved away, snorting fearfully. He brought the remembrance of death to them, the terror which had sprung from the benevolence of the lush marshes.

By sunrise the chestnut colt was dead.

6

For six months it hardly rained in the desert but somehow Blackface and his companions survived. By springtime they had found their way back to their old grazing lands and were there to drink from the water-hole before the stallion came back with his mares from the mountains. Black Legs was there with only one filly. The other, together with the colt sired by the sorrel, had been vanquished by winter and hunger together.

Led by the buckskin, the three of them attacked Black Legs and stole the filly from him, Blackface herding her off while the other two kept the stallion at bay, the pinto commanding his attention with exaggerated posturing and the buckskin actually charging in to do battle. Blackface had the filly to himself for only a very little while. She wasn't interested in his attentions, being heavily in foal, and only reluctantly allowed herself to be hazed away from the scene of battle. Very soon both the pinto and the buckskin came charging up and the buckskin made it clear straight away that the filly was his, flinging himself at Blackface without any warning and shouldering him to the ground. While the yellow colt struggled up again the buckskin attacked the pinto, screaming out threats as he pranced on hind legs over him. Both colts went for him and a three-sided skirmish developed, with as much noise as action. Meanwhile Black Legs came up and took the filly back.

When the bay stallion returned he chased them all off his

territory. Blackface and the pinto put up only a token display of courage before retreating. The buckskin replied to his threats with a brassy neigh of contempt, prancing forward to display himself, rearing up to full height to impress his ageing sire. The duel, however, was very brief for it needed great determination to resist the lightning kicks and bites with which the bay immediately responded, and the buckskin was still too much of a wanderer to care overmuch about territory. He retired pretty quickly, satisfied that his opponent knew his worth. Black Legs made off with his filly before any threats were offered. He couldn't afford to be drawn into battle and have her stolen from him again by the other three colts while he was distracted. Thus, on the same day as he returned, the bay stallion was once again in command of his domain.

Horses, plants, earth, all were waiting for the rain. Meanwhile they survived from day to day, as they had all winter through, and the colts kept away from the bay stallion's herd, most of their energy devoted to foraging.

It was different after the rains started. The mares began foaling again and coming into season and nothing could keep the young stallions very far away from them. Black Legs made a lightning foray into the herd while his own filly was foaling and came away with the grey mare's mahogany filly who was under the sorrel stallion's protection. The sorrel had three other fillies, a dun, a pinto and his sister, Pink Nose, to protect, so he chased after Black Legs for only a little way, afraid of losing the rest.

These young females were far more tempting to the outlaws than the bay stallion's mares, who were encumbered with foals or yearlings and protected by so dominant a stud, and it was only a matter of time before the sorrel lost them all. Black Legs got Pink Nose with a foal at foot, intercepting her return to the sorrel, and the buckskin ran off with the pinto filly and the dun after giving the sorrel a good kicking in the ribs and almost ripping off one ear. The bay stallion made no effort to protect him, feeling his years, conserving his energy.

The buckskin had gone his own way that summer, tired of trying to subdue Blackface and the pinto who, much as they fought with each other, always joined forces against him. However they soon became aware of the young stallion's new situation and trailed him constantly, determined to get the fillies from him if they could. These two young creatures behaved in a most capricious manner on coming into season for the first time. It was as if they were aware that every stallion around was interested in them and the prospect both frightened and excited them. They would alternatively accept and reject the buckskin's attentions; running away from him, trying to get back to their old companions; answering the love calls of both Blackface and the pinto with welcoming little squeals, much to their new master's fury. All his carefree spirit was gone now that he had these two fillies to defend, and he went around all day with his ears back and his eyes mean-looking, whinnying dire threats to his former companions.

Blackface did the challenging, approaching the buckskin in full display. Never had he lifted his legs so high as he pranced towards him, sideways on, that late afternoon, his thick black mane giving extra dimension to his well-arched neck, provocation and contempt expressed in the deliberate exposure of flank. The challenge roared out of him as the buckskin came galloping to meet him halfway, determined to keep him as far as possible from the two intensely curious and excited fillies, and he reared his highest, forelegs pawing the air.

They fought breast to breast, lunging at each other's neck and jaws, thrusting against each other's shoulders, striking at each other with both forelegs. Blood hot, their youth and contempt for each other made them impetuous in their rage and the battle was the hardest that either had ever fought. No sense of self-preservation tempered their actions; no remembrance of a long winter's companionship. Meanwhile the pinto made a wide detour and came snaking in on the fillies, surprising them into almost instant obedience. He hustled them away and not until they were well out of sight of the battling colts did he allow them to halt. Then he relaxed his tough stallion pose, encouraged them to come close to him, began nibbling at both in turn, all three exchanging little squeals of warning and pleasure.

Blackface came loping up to them later. There were several bites on his neck and withers, and grazes on his chest and haunches from kicks he hadn't been able to avoid, but his head and tail were raised in the stance of the victor. Warning snorts as he approached, ears pricked, eyes very bright, advised the pinto that his companion was in no mood to be hassled, so he gave up the fillies with good grace but kept very close to them all the same.

Now it was Blackface's turn to nuzzle and court them and the squeals, tail swishings, hoof stampings and nibblings began all over again. After a short while the pinto rejoined the group and, the heat of battle now gone from him, Blackface made no objection. He had soon discovered that two fillies were almost too much for him, anyway. While he busied himself with the pinto filly, the dun jealously attacked both of them. Her sudden kicks and bites were very distracting, and when Blackface angrily shouldered her away, the pinto had no difficulty in resuming his conquest of her.

The two colts shared their battle spoils without much quarrelling, their energy channelled into courtship. Several times the buckskin tried to get the fillies back but his attempts were only half hearted. He had already acknowledged Blackface's superiority and had no wish to tangle in a second battle with him. He maintained sufficient flight distance from the foursome but this didn't prevent either colt from pursuing him from time to time. They never chased him very far, being only too aware of the perils of leaving the two fillies unattended. The pinto did most of the chasing, Blackface already confident enough to keep the buckskin away with loudly whinnied threats. Black Legs made a couple of efforts to kidnap them but, with the buckskin colt still hanging around and the bay and sorrel stallions in the vicinity, he was more interested in defending the fillies he had rather than look for more.

7

The summer, with its storms and heat, passed away. Blackface and the pinto managed to hang on to their stolen females, mostly because between the two it was easy to defend them. The fillies had a rough time, being treated in much the same fashion as the colts the previous winter. The two stallions were very young, only four-year-olds, still more interested in proving their worth to themselves and each other than in settling down to the responsibilities of family life. Not for them just the business of guardianship and grazing. They were hecklers, firebrands, as eager as ever to flaunt their strength and virility before each other and any stallion within reach. They chased the fillies here and there, and when they were no longer in season hardly cared about them at all, except as subjects to be ruthlessly commanded.

In the heat-hazed afternoons, when at last they would be still for several hours, they still stood head to tail for comfort. They were still grooming partners and as strongly bonded to each other as in their early days. Instead of coming between them, the fillies had only strengthened their sense of unity, causing them to draw closer together in mutual defence. If there were any jealousies they were likely to be directed towards the females. Blackface would drive off a filly who might be trying to court the pinto's attention either for grooming or fly protection, and the pinto would do the same.

They were still no respecters of territory, poaching the bay stallion's if the grazing there was good; herding their fillies

right under the noses of Black Legs's little band in flagrant disregard of his irritation and possible retaliation; driving off the buckskin or any other lone colt, not because they felt threatened but from sheer high spirits and vainglory. The bay stallion ignored them once the breeding season was over. They never stayed long enough in one place to trouble him much, but Black Legs was still very sensitive about intruders and often gave chase. Then the two colts would gallop off, side by side, flanking the fillies, and first Blackface and then the pinto would halt to rear up with flailing hooves and brassy neighs of defiance before continuing their boisterous flight.

They were a turbulent, rambunctious pair the whole summer long, heedless of any authority but their own.

Summer didn't last, however. Day after day there was no more rain. The skies were blue and cloudless; the shadowless ground beneath grew harder and harder and began to crack. The wind blew dust into the horses' eyes, sweeping it from ground level into swirling dark columns and scattering it like rain. All the horses began to mooch about, blowing dismally through their nostrils as they searched in vain for a mouthful of fodder that might have been overlooked. They all knew it was time to move back to the *barranca*.

Again Blackface and the pinto remembered that warm, sheltered place and they stood for long periods with their heads lifted, pricked ears pointing westwards. The fillies did the same, for only last year they had wintered there under the sorrel stallion's protection. Every instinct urged them to return and for once they made up their own minds about where they would go, seeking out the bay stallion's band and their herd relations. The two colts followed and then took over, to keep the fillies in check.

The bay stallion's herd was already on its way and the little band of four trailed it eagerly. Black Legs must have had the same idea for both groups met while foraging among the trees at the top of the gorge. They kept at a mutually agreed distance from each other, taking it in turns to look down over the rim, anxious to follow the trail but, now they had got so far, remembering that the bay stallion was down there somewhere, determined to keep them away. The fillies were all very excited at meeting each other again and there was a lot of squealing and blowing until they settled down. When Black Legs decided to take his fillies somewhere else, he was careful only to go off with his own.

Urged by the two fillies, Blackface and the pinto went down into the *barranca*, stopping whenever they came to a place marked by the stallion as if wondering whether to continue. When they came to the valley, the stallion drove them away for the second time, but this year the colts didn't accept defeat so readily. True, they ran away, but the next day they were back and grazed close to the rocky entrance for some little time before the sorrel stallion caught sight of them and let out a loud neigh of alarm. They didn't wait for their sire to catch them but fled through the gap once more, grass hanging from their jaws, and for a while they were contented because their bellies were full.

Several times they did this, until all the grazing they could reach with impunity was exhausted. Then, like thieves who knew that no more could be taken from that particular property, they went away.

High above the gorge they searched for other valleys, just as they had the previous winter. At night the temperature was just above freezing point but during the day the sun was warm on their backs. They followed a rocky track that had once been a stream. It disappeared beneath a mass of prickly pear, oak shrubs and sumac bushes, but the horses forced their way through them for there was the damp scent of water in the air. Soon they could hear it, a faint trickle over stone, and the air grew colder as they came into the shadow of a three-hundred-foot rock from which a fine spray of water slipped and dripped into a small, dark pool at its base. From here the water drained into a short length of shallow stream which was quickly swallowed up by the tangled shrubs. The ground all about was marked with the tracks of the many different animals and birds that came to drink there but there were no lingering scents to frighten the horses.

It wasn't a bad place to be, at least not before the snow came. The grass was dry and yellow but it tasted good to the horses. They had to share it with mule-deer but they had seen these creatures before, in the bay stallion's valley, and weren't afraid of them. Their first encounter with a herd of wild black pigs was startling. All four horses bolted off in fright when the pigs came charging through the undergrowth like a swarm of mad hornets, with a smell so strong that for a long time afterwards the horses were still snorting and blowing, trying to rid their nostrils of it. The deer and pigs were the only daytime animals they ever saw but at night they heard the coyote singing to the moon and were fearfully aware of the passing of a cougar.

In the dark they slept close together, taking it in turns to keep guard. Rabbits, mice, skunks came to drink at the water-hole, cautious, fearful, only too aware of the bobcat or the cougar crouching in the shadows, and the dozing guard horse kept one ear well awake, distinguishing all the different animal sounds from the background whooshing of the wind. Many a night they were startled into racing off in the darkness without knowing quite what had frightened them.

On one of these occasions the pinto filly ran into the snapped-off branch of a pine tree. It drove straight into her chest, tearing flesh, skin, muscles, but reaching no vital organs. The wound was contaminated by bits of bark, moss, even splinters from the wood and, after a few days, too stiff to move any more, she lost her appetite and stayed by the pool, constantly thirsty as the poison in her body filled her with fever. A cougar cut short her suffering and soon the coyotes were quarrelling over her yellow and white hide and her bones. Blackface's unborn foal died with her.

When the snow came and the water froze and the day seemed as cold as night, the horses returned to the desert. They roamed as far as the marshes, where they grazed for a long time before being discovered and shot at again, but this time all three escaped unharmed. The dun filly was heavy with foal and no longer would she tolerate being herded about by the two young studs. To protect herself from them she grew so mean in temper that they were almost afraid to get near her, certain of being kicked or bitten, and so they left her alone for most of the day, preferring each other's company. She took them back to the bay stallion's territory as summer approached, the memory of the herd's birthing place strong within her.

When she was ready to leave them she made it quite clear that she wouldn't be followed or pushed around. Neither the pinto nor Blackface knew what to make of her but they did understand that she needed to be alone, reluctantly accepting this fact after being chased off several times when trying to bring her back. Then they forgot about her because the air was heavy with the scent of mares and fillies waiting to be claimed by the strongest stallion.

PART FOUR

King Stallion

I

For another two years Blackface and the pinto ran together, their partnership unaffected by the growing band of females they managed to gather. Whatever fillies they stole from other stallions, they shared with only token defiance of each other, and because of their relationship ·they were more successful than any other stallion in the area. Few could resist their combined attack; none could cope with their trick of dividing the fighting and stealing between them. Never was it necessary for them to leave their own herd unguarded and therefore at risk. They gained mares and fillies but lost none.

Black Legs lost three fillies to them, two greys and a bay; the buckskin battled hard to keep the only mare he had, a blue roan who was to become Blackface's favourite, and they kidnapped a chestnut filly with four white socks from a couple of young colts they met in their wanderings. The roan brought with her a yearling colt of the same colouring and a buckskin foal. These, together with the three foals sired by the two stallions, brought the herd's number up to twelve.

It was a lively herd, difficult to manage, composed almost entirely of youngsters, each equally jealous of establishing a good position for herself in the hierarchy. There was much chasing, kicking and biting among them over which the stallions had no control. Chances were that if either stud came among them to establish order they would be attacked and driven away, and so they learnt some lessons too.

Gone now were the days when they could race and roam at will, forgetful of all but the wind through their manes and the ground trembling under their hooves. If once their main purpose in life had been to hustle other stallions and steal females, now it was a continuous effort to defend and discipline a bunch of skittish, wilful creatures too young to know much about discipline or to have formed any serious bonds.

The chestnut filly had been in the possession of three different stallions before being kidnapped by Blackface and still she hankered for the close family unit of mother and younger brothers to which she had belonged for the best part of her life. It was the same with the rest. They all had memories of other loyalties and it took time for them to accept each other and discover their own worth. As overlords, Blackface and the pinto might control their wider destinies but their petty day-to-day relationships were altogether of their own making. All the studs could do was try to maintain some order amid the squabbling female disorder.

The blue roan mare finally brought peace and unity to the herd. An ugly creature, with every defect of conformation – head too big, body too thin, bones too prominent – she had the stamina of the very cactus and the speed of the wind. Her colouring was the only beautiful thing about her, being the blue of a stormy sky, of the mist-hazed mountains, of the shadows of rockfalls in the *barranca* – as changeable as she was steadfast. She took it upon herself to attack every filly in turn in a way that was as calculated as it was thorough.

First she picked on one of the greys as the weakest member of the herd and gave her such a kicking and mane-pulling that it left her nervous and spiritless for a week. Then she turned the same attention on the chestnut who, to get her own back, also attacked the already completely battered grey. It was the bay filly's turn next and, although she already started moving hurriedly away just at the sight of the roan's warlike advance, and rushed to attack the chestnut to give herself confidence and perhaps even gain some respite, the roan was equally merciless with her. Her hard hooves landed several times on haunch and belly and there was a chunk out of her withers almost before she realized it.

The second grey filly had been with the herd for a year. She had a foal by Blackface, which gave her a certain amount of authority as well as an extra reason for defending herself, and she replied to the roan's hectoring with menaces of her own. When threats and counter-threats produced no result, the two females attacked each other like stallions, squealing and rearing up, both foals watching wide-eyed and fearful not far away. The dun mare, who was now in her second year with the stallions and considered herself the boss of the herd, suddenly joined battle against the grey with jealous eagerness, anxious to help in the downfall of an enemy. Against two such opponents the grey's defeat was inevitable and in her turn she rounded on the lesser fillies, savage with resentment.

But the biggest battle, between the roan and the dun, was yet to come. For some time they kept away from each other, satisfying themselves with warning squeals and head tossings, until one afternoon the roan suddenly attacked, galloping straight up to the dun as she grazed unconcernedly and swirling at the last minute to unleash three lightning thumps into her ribs with both hind hooves before she could jump out of the way. The dun retaliated with strong kicks of her own and they rounded on each other with savage expressions of eyes and ears, squealing viciously as their hindlegs kicked again and again. Now one broke away to be pursued by the other and the rest of the herd watched with pricked ears, galloping out of the way as the two combatants scrambled among them.

Blackface and the pinto, excited by all the noise and movement, plunged amid the storming mares with much raising of dust, adding their own deep-throated whinnies to the noise. Both mares turned on them in a flash and kicked them out of the way before returning to the settling of scores, and in the end the dun fled away in defeat, to be rounded up and brought back by the pinto before she could go too far. After that there was peace among them. The blue roan and her younglings took first place at the water-hole, first place in the line, and the rest took up their respective positions behind. All the two stallions then had to do was watch over them, internal order being completely established without their assistance.

The two young studs no longer fought playfully with each other. Both were too busy guarding the herd, each in his own way considering himself entirely responsible for its well-being. The pinto watched and grazed in snatches on one side of the band, Blackface on the other and, except at watering times, they hardly came into contact with each other. In the afternoons, when the whole herd automatically drew close to doze and keep the flies away, they still maintained their positions on opposite sides of the herd, sometimes exchanging baleful glances if one believed the other to be trying to undermine his authority.

They were no longer grooming companions. The blue roan made a bee-line for Blackface every time he came into the herd. She was a great one for grooming and would often nibble and pull at one of the fillies against her will, keeping her submissive with threatening ears and even bites if she tried to get away. It seemed to be one of the ways she kept order in the herd for she rarely attacked any of them once they had accepted her authority, but every day she would choose one or the other to groom, making of the long-drawn-out process a punishment rather than a pleasure for the animal concerned because of the menace she exuded. With Blackface it was different. She came to him with submissive eagerness, rubbing her head against his cheek, her teeth reaching gingerly for his neck, uttering little squeals to which he replied with pleasurable snorts and head tossings. They would spend the whole afternoon side by side, nose to tail once the grooming was done, lower lips drooping, eyes closed, occasionally letting out a long sigh, the roan's buck-skin foal asleep on the ground not far away.

Thus the ties were gradually loosening between the two stallions, until there came a time when active resentment overtook their former tolerant acceptance of each other. While they stayed in one area there was no conflict but when-ever the band lined up for its daily trip to the water-hole, or to move to different grazing, the trouble began.

Both horses considered themselves the dominant member of the herd, entitled to hold the dominant flank position when they were on the move. As soon as the mares lined up, both Blackface and the pinto were alongside them to take com-mand. In the early days when there had been but few in the line they had moved in tandem quite happily, but now, with twelve animals to watch over, they were far more sensitive about their respective positions. Only one stallion could command the herd and day after day when the line-up took place each was reminded that the other vied for his position.

Every day they quarrelled. Blackface was the bigger animal and often the pinto would back down, only to lope to the front of the line and take over from the blue roan, or to swing round to the back and drive the herd ahead of him. Some days it would take a long time to reach their destin-ation because every time the stallions stopped to threaten each other the mares would draw aside to watch them, bewildered by this division of leadership.

For some time all they did was threaten, Blackface's fore-head pressed against the pinto's, eyes glaring at each other, almost in contact, pushing at each other like two stags locked together until one gave way. The minute the pinto backed down the quarrel was over. All Blackface wanted was to run alone, the acknowledged boss. They had fought many mock battles, each giving as good as he got, and perhaps because of this neither was anxious to press for a final showdown. The pinto broke away only to taunt his old companion from another key position, determined to keep mastership of the herd by trickery rather than strength.

Now and again they reared up in full display before either had taken up any position, the mares waiting for them to make up their minds. If the pinto made for the head of the herd, Blackface pursued him, the same as if he made for the back or the flank. He was only contented when he pushed himself in somewhere among the females, a position the pinto wouldn't tolerate for long. But for a long time they just blustered and bluffed and confronted each other with ritual displays of strength and token blows. They made a lot of noise, showed a lot of controlled rage, but steered clear of an ultimatum. While the pinto showed submissiveness Blackface tolerated him. While Blackface let him be the pinto believed he commanded the herd, but the more time went by the more he was reluctant to accept an inferior role. He was tired of ruling by stealth, of giving way, of being forced to run among the mares and fillies.

Summer and the new breeding season approached, adding to their natural belligerence. Each was as strong as he would ever be, rising eight years old, thick necked, hard muscled, short of temper and patience, gripped by the imperative drive to dominate instinctive to every stallion.

The day of reckoning started like all the rest, with the usual quarrel for the dominant flank position as they set off towards the water-hole at the end of the afternoon. The pinto got there first and when Blackface came up they locked their heads together as they snorted and squealed, pushing each other back and forth like two angry wrestlers. But although the pinto broke away it was only to return in a stronger attitude, this time determined to drive Blackface into the herd. Blackface wouldn't back down and for a while the two strutted and circled each other, snorting hard threats as they flaunted their strong heads and muscled chests, pounding the earth with iron hooves.

Blackface halted to confront the pinto head on, crashing one hoof to the ground in a violent gesture, as if he would thus crush the pinto were he close enough. In reply the other reared up and brought his legs crashing down even more violently. They squared each other up again, forgetting about position, forgetting about the mares, at last spurred to a confrontation which could give victory to only one of them. The years of shared hardship and fun were over.

Of one accord they attacked, not careful now of each other's body as in times gone by but clashing together with a hatred that can only be born of so long a kinship, big yellow teeth tearing wherever they encountered flesh to tear, desert-hardened hooves pounding against bone and muscle. They went down on their knees to strike cheek against cheek; they reared to their fullest height to thrust heavy blows wherever they might fall; they laboured shoulder against shoulder to rake each other's necks, flanks and back. They bit each other's legs and even resorted to backward kicking like the mares, and the noise they made sent rattlers and scorpions slithering under rocks to hide and wakened the bobcats from their slumbers.

Black Legs heard them and came to investigate, watching the two battling stallions from a distance. The mares, under the blue roan's watchful gaze, stood not far away, subdued by the fury of their masters. When the strange stallion started calling in their direction the blue roan drove them into a tight bunch and forced them to move on, out of his range. Blackface and the pinto broke out of their fight to chase after them but, moments later, seeing them all together, they slammed into each other again, breath rasping hard from their lungs. Both were tiring, without either seeming to gain the advantage, and for a moment they paused, continuing the battle with head-tossings and baleful expressions beyond reach of each other.

Then they pounded forward again, accompanying their last desperate flailings with echoing screams of fury, and suddenly the pinto staggered away, half concussed by a blow from Blackface's hoof that gashed him from ear to eye and blinded him with blood. He hardly knew what he was doing then, acting by instinct alone as he lowered his head to receive a further onslaught. But this action was enough for Blackface. He reared up to utter a lou.., throaty neigh of victory and by the time he had dropped to all fours the pinto was moving away, his action uncoordinated, still bewildered.

Blackface followed, grunting threats, his ears still flat, teeth showing. He pursued him like this for several minutes, until satisfied that the pinto had indeed accepted defeat, and then he turned and raced back to the mares, head and tail high, still unaware of the pain of his cuts and bruises, his body too hot and eager to start stiffening yet. He rounded them up with the most exaggerated of postures, head almost touching the ground, and when at last he had them moving towards the water-hole, flanking them at a canter, he let out a loud whinny of triumph which echoed across the desert to every stallion within hearing.

2

Three more foals were born to the herd that year, and for the first time since he had begun to gather females, Blackface was too busy caring for his own mares to go stealing any more. There were several young colts as well as Black Legs and the buckskin to guard against, and the pinto kept a distant watch on the herd, too.

Blackface was a most zealous overlord, keeping his females as close together as possible. This wasn't too difficult during the rainy season when grazing was reasonably plentiful but, as summer passed, the mares needed to search farther and farther afield to fill their bellies. They grew very recalcitrant, constantly breaking out of the small circle to which he confined them and answering his punishing nips with kicks. As soon as he brought one mare back another would be wandering off, sometimes several in different directions, so he learned to be more tolerant of their movements and took to watching over them from a greater distance to be more aware of the overall situation. With the pinto in the herd it had only been necessary to guard them on one flank. Now he had to learn how to keep watch on every side at once.

As winter approached it was necessary to find new grazing grounds. Blackface had given up trailing the bay stallion's herd to the *barranca*. For several winters now he and the pinto had gone eastwards to the marshes, in spite of the danger lying in wait for them there. They had learnt to flee at the first sight of any moving object, and for the last two years had grazed unmolested for most of the winter. Several bands of horses followed the same nomadic routes, some thirty animals in all, and occasionally they met and grazed together, although lone stallions were always kept at bay.

Blackface now had a herd of fifteen to watch over. He took them first to the mountains where there was grazing of one kind or another until the snows came and covered everything and then, driven back to the desert by cold and hunger, they began the long trek to the marshes. Days were spent searching for water. Some of the mares dug their own holes, others waited miserably for it to appear out of the ground, and the foals bleated hungrily because, without water, their dams had hardly any milk for them.

Two of the foals wandered into the fields of grusonia and lechugilla cactus. After gambolling carelessly along the narrow paths between clump and clump they suddenly found themselves trapped in a maze of spikes with no exits or entrances. They couldn't move without collecting legs full of needles and panic-stricken cries were exchanged between mares and youngsters unable to reach each other. A couple of hours went by before at last one of the foals saw a pathway and began to move, followed by the other. It was a chastening experience for them, painful too, as both had their legs punctured in many places before they were safe.

By the time they reached the marshes their hunger and thirst was such that caution was forgotten. They arrived as the sun was dipping into the desert, leaving mountains and marshes to a silver moon, and they grazed almost unceasingly for most of the night. At the approach of dawn Blackface gathered the mares together and drove them back to the desert, having learnt that death exploded in the daylight hours if it came at all.

The foals quickly fell asleep on the white, powdery gypsum, lulled by the sun on their hides, and the mares dozed watchfully near them. Blackface dozed for a little while too, after grooming and being groomed by the blue roan, but he was too restless and anxious to stay still for long. He climbed a high dune where saltbush and yucca grew in patches and from there had a good view over the whole area; shining lake with its upside-down reflection of the mountains, yellow marsh grass broken by dark shadows of stream and river, and the white-sanded desert with its bare, spidery ocotillo stretching skywards amid patchy green bushes. His black and yellow ears moved constantly back and forth, his dark eyes could see far things, his wide-flared nostrils identified every scent and there was no danger anywhere.

Blackface used this lookout point day after day and there was never anything to warn him that his mares could be in danger. They established a routine of grazing from dusk to dawn, covering over a mile of tufty yellow grassland before returning to the desert. The foals grew strong and chased each other about; the mares stayed thin but their hides shone in the desert sunlight.

Black Legs appeared with his troop of eight. The two stallions approached each other and then halted at a distance to make a ritual display of strength. Black Legs wasn't looking for conquests, only for grazing, and after a few minutes he turned his back on Blackface and cantered back to his herd. Within a few days the two families were grazing amicably almost side by side. The foals played and fought with each other and ran between the different mares indiscriminately, but at daybreak each family went its own way to rest. Neither stallion made any attempt to steal the other's females and the only time there was any trouble was when one of Blackface's yearlings went off with the other band by mistake. The two herds were almost half a mile from each other by the time Blackface realized what had happened. He hurtled after the other herd and recklessly dived in among the mares to seek his own colt. Black Legs was so surprised that before he could react Blackface was away, driving the terrified pinto colt before him, almost trampling him as he angrily chased him to where he belonged.

For weeks the two herds trespassed on the lakeside grass-lands, growing fat and sleek and contented, and then one morning before the sun was up they were ambushed by a bunch of cowhands who had planned this raid with the greatest of stealth and care. All through the night the men had come gradually upon the grazing horses, covering the last few miles on foot so that their own mounts shouldn't give them away, choosing a time of cloud and darkness, watching the wind. There were twenty of them, at least half armed with rifles or revolvers, and the first the wild herds knew of any danger was when a flock of birds flew up from the grass with loud cries just before dawn. At this, the rifles began to crack and, even before they could spring into a gallop, mares and youngsters were collapsing into the grass with thrashing legs, whinnying out screams of pain.

In a moment the two stallions were streaking round their herds, instinctively gathering them into one big bunch to flee in greater safety, but against this unnatural enemy, swift and invisible, there was no protection and those still on all fours collided with their stricken companions, still not knowing from where the danger came.

Blackface raced alongside the mares, Black Legs bringing up the rear, making for the desert and its silent safety. The men began to show themselves, waving their arms and shouting, fearsome-looking creatures caught by the first rays of the new morning's sun as they stood between the horses and the desert, barring their way. Eyes wild with the terror that screamed in their throats, the leading mares wheeled away from them, back towards the guns, heedless of Blackface's authority as he plunged biting among them but as bewildered as they were.

Black Legs didn't follow. Instead he galloped towards the line of men in desperate rage, ears flattened, teeth bared, so

frightening in aspect, demented by fear, that the men began to run out of his way to let him pass. But the grey stallion was blind to the desert just ahead, blind to all but the enemy he could at last see. His head stretched out as he closed in on the nearest cowhand, teeth ready to tear, but several bullets, fired in unison, tore through his lungs and heart and brought him down.

Meanwhile Blackface had been fighting to turn the mares back to the desert, and these few moments of distraction were enough for the horses still on their legs to flash through the broken barrier, the men still firing after them although they couldn't follow. For a long time they galloped on and on until at last they could go no further, eyes glazed with the agony of their overstrained hearts and lungs. Then they halted and stood without moving, heads almost touching the ground, blind, deaf, utterly exhausted. Just then any enemy could have finished them off and they wouldn't have known where death had come from, but apart from cacti, scorpions, beetles and rattlesnakes they were the only living things beneath the sun.

3

Of the twenty-five horses that had grazed the marshes, only six escaped with Blackface to the desert. Of these, three died over the next few days from a combination of wounds and exhaustion. All that remained were the blue roan mare from Blackface's band and two of the grey stallion's mares, Pink Nose and his full sister, the mahogany mare. Each of them had lost a foal and when their senses had come back to them they whinnied plaintively for their missing younglings. Blackface kept them moving away from the marshes but only their overriding fear of the terror they had escaped made them obey him. They knew the foals had been left somewhere behind them and would now and again halt and gaze in that direction, ears pricked with longing. Blackface drove them relentlessly on. It took them a long time to recover from so fearful an experience and any bird cry was sufficient to set them off at a gallop without pausing to consider its cause.

By springtime they were back on their old grazing grounds, the three mares heavy with foal, and Blackface was searching the wind for the scent of young fillies. The bay stallion was back, too, still commanding the biggest herd. He had only three mares now, the grey, White Patch and the sorrel, and a couple of youngsters, while the sorrel stallion had four fillies, two yearling colts he had sired and several foals, in all numbering fourteen. The buckskin stallion and the pinto were still around, and still bachelors. They had joined forces and were therefore formidable opponents for the herd stallions, though more attracted to the bay stallion's band than Blackface's because of the fillies coming into season for the first time.

The bay had grown in artfulness over the years and, although he was still a tough and fearless battler, if he could escape with his mares without having to fight for them he preferred to do so. He thrust out his colts when they were only yearlings, saving himself the problem of having to discipline two-year-olds, and left it to the sorrel to defend his daughters. That summer the sorrel stallion was involved in more battles than ever in his lifetime, staying behind to outface the attackers while the bay stallion ran off with the herd. He was a hardy twelve-year-old and his unwillingness to defend himself as a youngster, except in flight, had turned into a stubborn refusal to be pushed aside.

He would stand and fight and then run off just as soon as he calculated that the mares were safe, and the next day he would be ready to face the buckskin or the pinto again, bouncing back from every retreat with renewed vigour. His enemies were disconcerted by this behaviour and after a while began to keep out of his way, trying to gain a direct approach to the bay stallion but finding the sorrel always barring their path.

That summer no mares or fillies were kidnapped, Blackface being too busy defending his little herd from the hungrily persistent studs to do any stealing for himself. But he watched the bay and sorrel's families with longing whenever they were within sight.

Once the breeding season was over and he could relax his vigilance a little – but never altogether because the buckskin and the pinto were never very far away – Blackface began to take an interest in his foals. At first he just watched the two colts as they played together, repeating all the processes that had once so engrossed him and the pinto in their foalhood.

He was intensely curious and occasionally – when the mood took him – he would slowly pace up to them, abandoning all dignity, pricking his ears and snorting with all the friendliness of any youngster eager to join the game.

The first time he did this the foals, sons of Pink Nose and the blue roan, had been terrified. They ran to their dams for protection, then, safe at their sides, lifted their cheeky heads to stare boldly at him, big ears stiff with anticipation. Blackface uttered a few sociable snorts but didn't pursue them. He stood where he was, head half lowered, black tail half lifted, offering himself for a game. After a while they learned not to be afraid of him and then when he came up to them they would race in mad circles round him, legs kicking, heads tossing, no doubt considering themselves very fine and brave. The mahogany mare's filly foal interested him less. He nibbled her neck and withers a few times but her dam was excessively protective towards her and generally kept him at bay, her malevolence inherited from her mother.

Between the mahogany mare and the blue roan there was a great deal of jealousy, both competing for the leading position even though the herd only numbered three. Pink Nose was as mild as her sorrel dam and kept out of the way of both of them, but hardly a day passed when the two dominant mares didn't attack each other with bites or kicks. The roan's trick of trying to dominate through the grooming relationship had no effect on her. Whenever she came up with her bossy grooming expression her rival would retaliate by throwing up her head and baring her incisors. Now and again the mahogany mare paired up with Pink Nose in the afternoons, but the blue roan attacked her whenever she found them grooming each other, giving Pink Nose a few kicks into the bargain if she couldn't get away in time. Blackface still favoured the roan and sometimes, after they had spent an hour side by side dozing in the sun and nibbling each other, he would join with her in attacking her rival, but

even then the mahogany mare wouldn't concede the leadership.

Whenever they were on the move they tussled the whole
way, lunging at each other's faces or necks, ears flattened,
expressions wicked, their foals skittering along unconcernedly
beside them while Pink Nose calmly brought up the rear
and ignored them. Blackface didn't always defend the roan.
If he considered that their squabblings were holding up or
endangering their progress he would attack whichever mare
happened to be nearest to him. At the water-hole the two
jealous females spent more time trying to keep each other
away than actually drinking.

At last one day they fought it out in a screaming, biting,
kicking battle. Both mares were evenly matched and either
could have won except that the mahogany mare was un-
fortunate enough to find herself cornered by a wall of prickly
pear into which she had inadvertently backed. She panicked
on finding her escape cut off and made a frantic leap over
the lowest plants, getting one hoof caught and only half
clearing them. Hundreds of needles plunged into different
parts of her body, sending her mad with irritation. She
dashed off, kicking and bucking, biting at herself, and was so
crushed with misery for days that even Pink Nose could bull-
doze her about. She did so much rolling, rubbing and biting
that her hair came out in patches, making her a sorry sight,
and by the time most of the spines had worked their way out
the roan was well established as lead mare. Even then she
acknowledged the other's authority with bad grace, always
retaliating with a threat before backing down, but at last
there was order in the herd again.

Blackface was thinner that year than in any of his whole
life, made excessively nervous by the marshland massacre
and forced into numerous skirmishes by the bachelor studs
who never gave up trying to steal his mares from him. The
most solid parts of him were his head and neck which, with

his tangled black mane, looked almost too heavy for the rest of his sparse, mottled, oatmeal frame. His movements were almost as constant as a bird's for, although he might stand for long periods in the same position, his gaze was never still and all his body was working in its different ways to identify scents, sounds and far-distant objects. Never would his head drop to graze for more than a few moments at a time. As soon as his teeth had ripped a mouthful of grass or twigs his head would jerk up while his jaws crunched and a minute or more might pass before he lowered it again. But still he was as hard as the very desert rocks and as deadly in his tyrannous protection of his herd as any rattlesnake facing danger.

Before the summer was over both the buckskin and the pinto would move away when, spying them from a distance, Blackface reared up and neighed loud and clear his challenge to them. They had permanently marked his body in several places with their teeth and hooves, but at last they left him alone.

4

The last of the summer rains had fallen. Several weeks had passed since the sky had been overcast with heavy thunder-clouds and half a year would pass before they came again. The agave flowers had spread their seeds and withered, the chino grama grass had all been eaten, the yellow paper flowers might never have existed. Only the cacti, standing out stiffly from the stark earth, stayed the same regardless of rain or drought, heat or cold.

Blackface's mares wandered about, noses to the ground, with an air of despondency. The foals were happy enough, their bellies still round with milk, but their dams were hungry. They nibbled the leaves from every mesquite bush, stripped the bark and twigs from the branches, and were hungry. The bay stallion's band had already gone to its mountain retreat, followed by the pinto and the buckskin, so that Blackface and his family had most of this desert territory to themselves. They gleaned from it every last mouthful and spent a lot of time nosing carefully among the fallen prickly pear pads, looking for those that had lost their spines. When they were hungry enough they chewed at the tough, fibrous joints still intact, mouths and tongues hardened against the myriad prickles, but all of them were restless to move somewhere else.

Many times did Blackface gaze eastwards, remembering the lush lakeland marshes, but it was in the opposite direction that he finally turned with his mares and colts, making for the bay stallion's *barranca*. They stopped to water at the stream and to allow the foals to rest and, while the mares pulled hungrily at the grass and bushes round about, Blackface stood at the rim of the canyon, looking down into it with pricked ears, the wind tugging against him. They stayed at this place for several days. It was very cold, the night temperatures dropping well below zero, the heavy fogs frosting bushes, plants and stone. Until the sun came to melt it away there was nothing for the horses to eat because even the bark on the trees was frozen.

Blackface led them to the place where the wild pigs rooted and here they stayed until the snow came, snorting with fear and galloping madly away whenever the pigs scuffled or charged through the bushes, quivering at night as a cougar prowled nearby. The pinto and the buckskin turned up one day and Blackface chased them off with furious squeals, aware that in this steep and wooded terrain they might easily make off with one of his mares.

They resisted the snow until the softly falling flakes became blinding whirlwinds of bitter ice and the drifts were hock deep. Then they toiled back to the *barranca*, coats matted with ice, legs weak with weariness, and after only momentary hesitation Blackface led his mares and foals down to the bay stallion's valley. The water was colder than it had ever been and the way was no longer exactly as he remembered it for there had been rockfalls in one place, and in another their passage was almost blocked by driftwood brought down by the river in flood.

Reluctantly the mares struggled on, hampered by the foals who were verging on complete exhaustion. But the ice had melted from their coats and although the day was grey and chill it was warmer than they had known it since they left the desert. There was some respite for them when they came to the little beach. The foals suckled and slept but Blackface was nervous and anxious and several times plunged into the water as if to encourage the others to move. The mares ignored him, taking the weight off each leg in turn as they stood with half-lowered heads and dropped ears and waited for their foals to recover. They spent the night grazing on the steep slope near the entrance to the rocks that hid the bay stallion's valley from them, and by sunrise the foals were so much recovered from their exertions that they experienced many a tumble as they bounced about, unable to control their balance on the almost perpendicular ground.

When Blackface drove his mares that morning into the bay stallion's valley his only intention was to find them secure grazing for the winter. The last time he had eaten of that grass was years earlier, when he and the pinto as colts had snatched quick mouthfuls and then run, but now his days of running were over and he was as hungry as his mares. Even so, his mood was not a belligerent one. He was wary but self-confident, after no conquests, making no claims, and he set to grazing with the avidity of the others just as soon as the grass was there beneath their hooves.

Very soon the other stallions and their mares became aware of the intruders. They were near the pool, among the acacia and kapok trees, and for a while they all just stared, ears pricked, heads high. There were restless snorts and throaty whickers and the sorrel stallion uttered a hostile squeal. Blackface and his band stared back but, as no movement was made towards them and their bellies still clamoured, the mares soon fell to grazing again, hunger greater than curiosity or fear. Blackface, however, took a few paces forward, tossing his head and returning a squeal of his own. It was not so much a challenge as a warning to be left alone.

But now the sorrel stallion was trotting towards him, lifting his legs high, flexing his neck muscles, full of bluff and bluster, backed by righteous indignation. The bay stallion watched but didn't move. He was weary of battles and if he still maintained the dominant place in the herd it was mainly because the sorrel had not yet been moved to dispute it with him. He was much scarred and there was an ache in his bones from their many bruisings. Perhaps only a year ago he would have been prancing forward instead of the sorrel, ready to drive Blackface from his domain, but now, had he not had the younger stallion to defend him, the chances were he would have let Blackface and his mares share the valley with him rather than risk losing it altogether, putting off his defeat for another occasion.

The sorrel was at full maturity, his confidence bolstered by several years of near command. He had spent most of the previous summer successfully outbluffing the pinto and the buckskin and perhaps because of this he judged his new opponent in the same light. He had never had to defend the mares in the valley before and therefore didn't take into account the fact that his desert tactics, standing for a while and then running, would be of no use because here there was nowhere for the mares to escape to. He didn't understand, either, that Blackface hadn't come to steal his mares, that all he wanted was to be allowed to graze in peace.

He halted a few lengths off and began a display of strength, rearing, pawing the air, his neigh echoing round the valley, and the mares behind him drew together with their colts as was their custom. Blackface replied in the same fashion but because he wasn't offering any challenge, only letting the other know that he was not to be underrated, he then turned aside, prepared to go back to his grazing.

His challenger interpreted this movement as an acknowledgement of defeat and, ears flat, dashed towards him, ready to press home his advantage with a few meaningful bites. Blackface swirled to face him again, taking him by surprise. The sorrel pulled up sharply, jerking back his head as the other plunged on hindlegs towards him, and met one of Blackface's flailing hooves sideways on, which stunned him for a second or two. Blackface tore into him, aggressiveness unleashed, and the sorrel, staggering backwards, was forced into a defensive position which always triggered off his instinct to flee.

Blackface chased after him, roaring out his rage. The mares, together with the bay stallion, were already racing up the valley but their way was abruptly terminated by the narrowing of the *barranca* walls where only the river could pass over the tumble of rocks. Brought up sharply, they turned to watch the sorrel who was obliged to confront Blackface or back down altogether.

Not ready for defeat, he fought back, but with more bluff than effectiveness. Under pressure, he broke off to escape once more. Blackface followed him the length of the valley and back, getting in a blow or a bite whenever the sorrel tried to retaliate, winning all the way in the more favourable role of pursuer and squealing out his triumph. His hard black forelegs imperiously stamped the ground as he defied the sorrel to return to the attack then, impatient of his reluctance, he flung himself at him once more. At this point the bay stallion intervened. His nature was as fiery and volcanic as ever, undiminished by age though more controlled and, having left the mares in a bunch at the far end of the *barranca*, he plunged into the attack with all his old fury, making a shoulder rush at Blackface as he went for the disadvantaged sorrel and warning him of his approach with a trumpeting roar.

With the bay stallion to back him the sorrel was more prepared to stand his ground, perhaps understanding too, by this time, that there was nothing to be gained by escape. There would never be another day on which to continue the only battle he had ever instigated. Everything must be won or lost today, and he countered his enemy's rush with flailing hooves.

Blackface was disconcerted by this double attack. He had

the strength of one and the experience and cunning of the other to contend with. Staggering and almost falling under the impact of the bay's shoulder crashing against his own, and only just escaping the sorrel's hooves, he gave quite a bit of ground, rapidly backing off in a daze. But within moments he rallied and charged at the pair of them, jaws wide, hooves thrashing, a whirlwind of hammer blows and screams.

Never had the valley known such noise and confusion as the three-sided battle went on. The birds flew off or hid in the rushes; the soft-eyed deer bounded from one side to another to keep out of the way; and the two groups of mares, together with their youngsters, watched and waited, Blackface's half-starved band snatching at the grass in the meantime. So close was the scrimmage that at times the blows of the sorrel and the bay landed on each other instead of on Blackface.

The sorrel couldn't endure such sustained violence. He broke away and fled with every appearance of defeat, neck and shoulders bloody with wounds. Blackface freed himself from the bay to race after him, driving him towards the exit from the valley with such speed and menace – neck low and elongated, teeth sinking into legs and fetlocks at every opportunity – that the sorrel was too intimidated to care for anything but flight. The bay chased after the pair of them and, even as the sorrel fled through the fissure in the rocks, scattering the intruding mares and colts at his panic-stricken approach, the bay caught up with Blackface unawares, battering into him with vicious hooves. Blackface fell back under this new onslaught but he was quicker to react than the bay, returning a flashing attack with unexpected speed.

Both were utterly weary, with no energy left for rearings and proud displays. Their sweat-soaked bodies were marked in many places and their throaty challenges were lost while they blew and heaved and struggled for their second wind, extended nostrils showing pink. For a time they were reduced to straining against each other like two stags, black forelocks intermingled, both giving and gaining ground, neither admitting defeat. Then they went down on their knees and battled mouth against mouth, splitting each other's lips. Blackface sprang up faster than the bay stallion, in his weariness turning to kick back at him like a mare, his hooves catching the bay full in the face as he pushed himself up.

The bay stallion could take no more but he was either too exhausted or too proud to run. He just stood there, head low, mouth open, while Blackface snorted threats and wearily stamped the ground, raising and lowering his head menacingly but equally spent. He could no more drive his opponent off than the bay stallion could be driven. For a time they faced each other, Blackface's head movements and snortings dying away when the bay stallion gazed in another direction as if to show that he wasn't interested in him any more, sanctioning his presence there. Then Blackface did the same and when each was ignoring the existence of the other the bay stallion turned and began to move away, limping as the weight of his years and the pain of his wounds, new and old, overcame him.

By now, sensing that all hostilities were over, the mares had broken out of their tight bunch and were grazing again, unconsciously separating themselves into their respective family groups, close but not intermingled. The bay, as if to reassure himself, drove round his own group, lunging bad-temperedly at his mares and taking them back to the lakeside, careless of the sorrel's abandoned family which he left at the far end of the *barranca*. For the rest of the day he hardly moved from the shade of the kapok trees, stiff and weary.

Blackface, lamed by a rapidly swelling stifle, eventually returned to his mares, too, going from one to the other to sniff and nuzzle and satisfy himself that everything was well with them. Then he began to graze. The deer settled down and the birds came back and the valley was peaceful once more. A couple of days later, though still very lame, Blackface travelled the length of the valley to investigate the sorrel's family which kept together under the leadership of the dominant filly. After a lot of snorting and squealing, he rounded them up and drove them back to his own band. The bay stallion watched but didn't interfere.

5

Blackface's band now numbered thirteen, while all that remained to the bay stallion were his three old mares and the three colts he had sired over the last couple of years. They shared the valley amicably enough for the rest of that winter, careful not to meet at the pool or anywhere else, both reluctant to instigate further clashes in so confined a space.

The sorrel stallion several times tried to regain his fillies, slipping back through the rocks and whickering hopefully to them before dashing off at Blackface's rocketing approach. He grew very thin, refusing to leave the *barranca*, finding next to nothing to eat, and then not even able to leave because of the snow. Desperation forced him to return to the valley again and again to snatch quick mouthfuls of grass before being spotted. When he stopped calling the mares and made off just as soon as Blackface lifted his head to watch with pricked, imperious ears, life became easier for him. Blackface tired of chasing him and, as long as the sorrel was suitably submissive, was prepared to let him graze.

Blackface left the valley before the bay stallion, impatient for movement again once the best of the grazing was spent. It had been his best winter for many a year and his vigour was too much of a fire within him to be contained in so small an area. His was a young herd and, even though the mares and fillies were beginning to feel the weight of their unborn foals, they were soon infected by his excitement, as eager to be off as he was. The sorrel followed at a distance, halting whenever Blackface looked in his direction, very discreet but never entirely without hope, a hanger-on from first to last.

Blackface kept off the bay stallion's desert territory for, with the coming of the rains, there was sufficient grazing everywhere. The most he did was claim first rights at the water-hole which meant that whenever his band approached any horse that happened to be there had to move off and wait until it had left. The first time he confronted the bay stallion at the water-hole it seemed he might have to establish his right by force, for the old horse was loth to give way. Blackface put on a show of fury and the bay backed down. His grey lead mare showed more spirit, ready to dash away even as she purposefully went on drinking, and kicking out backwards as Blackface's blue roan bulldozed towards her with flattened ears and bared incisors.

That season the bay stallion lost all his mares to various studs who, aware now of his failing strength and no longer respecting him, made merciless attacks. At one time he could have warded off would-be kidnappers several times a day and still found the energy to drill his mares at a gallop but now, although he fought valiantly when brought to bay, he no longer had the stamina to win. Blackface, too, had a hard time defending his mares and fillies, for the available fillies were fast dwindling in number and he possessed most of them. The size of his herd was increased by the six foals born to it, three of them sired by the sorrel, but in spite of his efforts he lost the mahogany mare's filly to the pinto stallion who plagued him with the persistence of a hornet until at last he made off with a prize.

It was Blackface's tenth summer and he was as strong as ever the bay stallion had been in his prime, possessor of the biggest herd but already with sons of his own coming of an age to harry if not endanger him. In those ten years as many mustangs had been lost as had been born, so that now, in all that hard desert area, there were perhaps no more than three dozen survivors, not enough to save them from extinction.

For another ten years Blackface remained the dominant stallion, siring colts and fillies as wild as himself, including two golden palominos with all of his own dam's beauty but none of her gentleness. There was no man to covet them and so they remained free, bound only by the rigours of their natural life, hunger, heat, cold and thirst. Blackface fought many a battle over those ten years to keep both his mares and his territory, and he grew as wise as his sire, learning when it was expedient to withdraw rather than accept a challenge, discovering that strength and courage were not always as powerful as cunning or patience. They were his best years. With the *barranca* valley to retire to each winter, his survival and that of his mares and colts was ensured. He sired some forty colts and fillies but less than half of them survived their first five years, many of them losing their lives on the marshes, victims of man's constant encroachment on the wilderness.

It was man who eventually closed the valley to them. There were many valuable minerals in the Sierra Madre – iron, lead, zinc, gold, silver, copper – and the search for new mining areas eventually led engineers and technicians to that unmolested *barranca* where one summer their dynamite blew holes in the rock face and brought boulders tumbling to the river in minutes when, before, centuries of wind and rain had been required to move them. The river continued to flow as it always had but when Blackface led his mares and colts down into the gorge for the eighth successive winter, their usual fording place beyond the little beach was blocked by giant stones around or over which they could find no passage.

He knew there was no other way into the valley but still he sought one, making the mares and foals struggle through deep as well as shallow pools, risking their legs and hooves on painfully unsure ground, with next to no grazing to console their wet and battered bodies. Eventually he took them up into the mountains where they survived until the snow drove them back to the desert. That winter three foals died, too much weakened by cold and hunger and perhaps not as inherently strong as the foals of young-blooded animals, and the energy of the whole herd was drained by its constant wandering search for food and water. Blackface would not take them back to the marshes and by the time the spring rains came their endurance had been tested to the utmost. Pink Nose died foaling an awkward colt under the tree where Blackface had been born.

In spite of the hard winter Blackface was as alert as ever to defend his herd from plundering colts and stallions, driving off his young fillies in an effort to keep their dams safe. With the fillies to fight over and steal from each other, the marauders were often kept occupied enough and too wearied by battles with each other to force more than half-hearted encounters with a stallion whose aggressiveness most of them had good cause to remember. However, they harried him a good deal whether their intentions were serious or not, all of them as gaunt as he was but with only half his battle scars.

Blackface's affection for the blue roan mare endured. She was still his favourite grooming partner, partly because in her jealousy she would allow no other mare close enough to him for any length of time, viciously driving off any that seemed to court his attention unduly. She was jealous of all the in-season mares, attacking them and their foals, and as she grew older she grew meaner so that, had it not been for Blackface, she would have dozed in the afternoons' fly-plagued heat all alone. She produced a foal every other year and the eldest of these, a mottled dun with a face as black as his sire's, was Blackface's most persistent challenger in his later years.

Every year after his first outlawed summer he was around

to tease and taunt, sometimes running alone, sometimes joining up with several younger colts which he ruthlessly commanded, and eventually, in his seventh year, engaging Blackface in one of the hardest battles of his life. By then he had twice his sire's resistance but only half his experience and Blackface wouldn't be drawn into the encounter until his rival was almost completely unnerved by his own daring.

With the valley sealed off from all the horses there were as many quarrels over winter grazing as there were for mares. Blackface claimed the place of the wild pigs for his band – one of the best because of its water supply, but also dangerous because the water that attracted so much wild life also brought predators in train. The foals were particularly at risk to a prowling cougar that could wait hours on a tree branch, hidden in the foliage, watching for a youngster to frisk and gallop far from its dam. Blackface did his best to keep the herd together but such difficult terrain forced them to graze in scattered fashion, often out of sight of each other. The foals were easy and tempting prey here where their speed was of no use to them. In one winter all the colt foals were lost, the fillies surviving because they were less adventurous than their brothers, staying closer to their dams.

They ate the bark off the trees and nibbled the mesquite bushes bare once the snow had covered the ground and left them without any grazing, and when obliged to return to the desert they subsisted as best they could on prickly pear, wandering for many miles in search of something better. The winds that drove across that bleak terrain brought an ache to Blackface's ageing bones, so often bruised in battle, and there were days when he was very lame. There were deep sockets above his eyes and his teeth were much worn by the hard fodder that had been his lot for many a year.

The following summer the mottled dun pursued him again, roaring out his challenge in a voice that echoed Blackface's youth. The old stallion bunched up his mares and drove them deeper into his own territory but the mottled dun was used to his tactics now and galloped along beside them, trying to command them from the other flank. Then he took the lead, intending to swing them away from Blackface, and the mares instinctively followed, unaware of his intentions.

This was too much for Blackface who, putting on an extra burst of speed, flung himself after the mottled dun with a cry of rage, teeth bared for action. The racing mares collided with the pair of them and scattered in several directions, collecting again and watching from a distance while the two stallions fought it out. The mottled dun had all the advantages – youth, strength, self-confidence – and although he was rag thin every muscle of his body functioned like a well-oiled steel spring. There was little elasticity left in Blackface, not enough to save him from the lightning kicks and slashes of the other nor to resist the pounding of his blows. His spirit was still all steel and fire, however, and it was this that kept him face to face with his overpowering rival who dodged most of his blows, demolished his defences, and cared nothing for his slashing teeth.

He fought Blackface to a standstill, unable to make him run, and while the old stallion almost rocked on his legs in an exhausted daze, hardly able to see, he snaked round the mares with a victorious whistling cry and took command. They were loath to move at first, having run many years with Blackface, and he had to bite at their withers and legs to get them started. Blackface was still hardly any distance away but he was deaf to their calls of distress. The blue roan gave her new master a hard kick in the chest before jumping away from his punishing teeth, and then she broke from the bunch he had formed, wheeling back to Blackface who still stood motionless with drooping head. The dun came after her, head almost touching the ground, snorting and squealing fiery threats, but she refused to be herded back to the rest, eventually galloping off in the opposite direction with defiance in her bucking heels.

Disconcerted by her wilfulness, afraid of losing the others if he went in pursuit of her, the mottled dun finally decided to make do with the battle spoils within reach, which included four mares and a dozen youngsters. He gave them a hard drilling, keeping them on the run in constantly changing directions until he was sure they accepted his command, and then he came in among them to court them, exchanging squeals and grunts, offering caresses to the sweating, excited and half fearful mares, giving sharp nips to the youngsters to keep them in their place – above all triumphant.

6

Blackface recovered from the mottled dun's ravaging attack though his whole body ached. The scents in the wind told him where his mares were grazing but he was old enough to know when he was defeated. As a colt he would have followed them across the desert and back again, expectancy undiminished, but just now he didn't care. The rain eased the cuts and swellings on his body, the hot sun soothed them, and if his old injuries were aggravated by this latest battle he was used to lameness by now and patient.

The blue roan mare came back to him, made nervous by her solitary state, however short it had been, and they groomed each other thoroughly and swished the flies from each other's chest and flank. They stayed together, keeping well away from other stallions. Blackface was still spirited enough to defend the only mare left to him from the tentative attacks of the few young colts that occasionally trailed them, and still strong enough to dig holes in the ground for water. The roan foaled a colt which was an exact replica of herself, and Blackface waited patiently for her only a hundred yards away, head lifted, ears pricked, eyes alert for any danger. For several days she wouldn't allow him near the colt, driving him off whenever he approached too close for her liking, but she received his attentions with all her old affection before the week was out. For lack of any other playmate, the colt persistently brought Blackface into his games, wrestling with the old stallion's head and sometimes getting hurt.

As autumn approached the three of them made for the place of the wild pigs, grazing on the stony hillside amid the oaks and pines, often only half visible to each other in the mists that hovered between earth and sky. Later the mottled dun turned up with the mares and youngsters that were now his, pugnaciously driving the firstcomers away. With the roan behind him, Blackface climbed higher and higher into the mountains, following the paths of big-horn sheep where they were not too steep or rocky, otherwise making his own while snatching at patches of grazing wherever it could be found.

One morning, as he skirted a rocky incline, following it round a blind bend, he came face to face with a trapper. Never had he been so close to man before and he reared up with a snort of fear to dash away. The trapper was as startled as the stallion and his reaction was as instinctive as it was rapid. Even as the hooves flashed above him, giving him a glimpse of black-lined belly, his revolver was out and exploding hardly six feet from the stallion's chest.

Blackface's snort was cut off as his body crashed into the gully bordering the narrow track and the trapper never even saw the blue roan and her colt, with such speed did they whirl and dash away. But he heard the scream of fear that was rent from her as the sound of his gun vibrated through ears and memory, and he heard their galloping hooves. He looked down into the gully, where Blackface's body had come to rest amid a tangle of mesquite bushes, still only half aware of what had happened. Then, with a shrug of his shoulders, he put his gun away.

The blue roan put a lot of distance between the echo of the gunshot and herself before coming to a halt, caring only that the colt was beside her, his movements an extension of her own. When at last she halted she was still in unknown territory, though heading for a place she knew, but she let the colt suckle before moving on, her pace slower but still

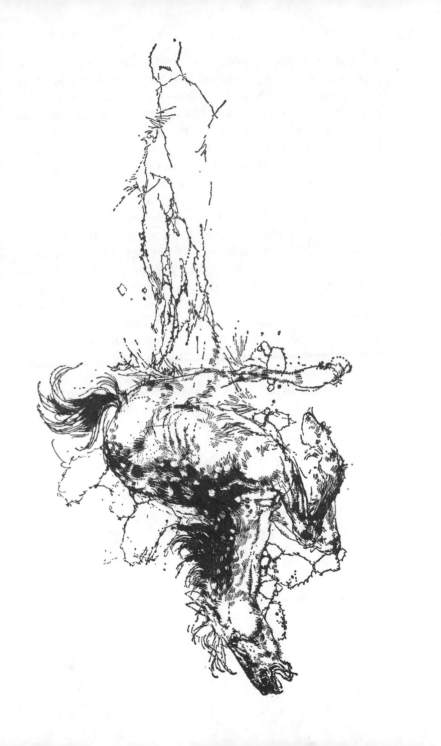

anxious. She didn't look back for Blackface; she knew that he was gone. Her first instinct was to protect her youngling. There was nothing else to guide her but this.

It took her several days to reach the place of the wild pigs, where the smell of her old companions reached her long before she could see them among the trees and bushes and, though she was anxious to be among them, once she was within calling sound of them she halted. She was an outsider, no longer one of them.

The colt was all eagerness to go forward and he cavorted and reared, snorted and shook his proud little head, impatient of his dam's caution. He ran rings round her, trying to tease her into movement, but she stood expectantly and ignored him, waiting for the herd boss to find her. A little while went by because the wind's direction didn't favour a quick discovery, but eventually the mottled dun got the scent of her and with his sire's own quick and haughty pace came trotting up, blowing with eagerness. He no longer remembered her defiance of him when he had stolen the rest of Blackface's mares, and he uttered short squeals of command and welcome, black ears working back and forth, tail lifted high.

The colt had shrunk into her flank, all arrogance gone at the sight of this powerful stallion, almost the image of the stud that had sired them both. The mottled dun came pushing into him with his nose and the foal made suckling noises from fright as his dam turned her head towards him, flattening her ears at the stallion in malevolent warning. But she needed no urging this time when he lowered his head to drive her into his herd.

She went with head high, ears pricked, a battling expression in her eyes, ready to wrest the leadership from whichever mare happened to hold it, fighting for her colt as much as for herself. And the long-legged, dappled blue foal pranced along beside her, suddenly fearless again, eager to know new things, new playmates with whom today's games would become tomorrow's battles if ever any of them survived the gradual encroachment of man into this very last retreat.

The mottled dun stallion, his face as black as his sire's, his young body as hard forged and confident, his spirit as free and unbreakable, watched the first wary greetings and scuffles among the mares. Then he looked away over the hillside; nostrils wide stretched, eyes alert; leaving them to their own business. His was to guard them while they grazed and dozed, quarrelled and gave birth, year after year.